RADGEPACKET

Tales from the Inner Cities

Volume Three

A collection of short fiction from around Great Britain.

Featuring

Danny King
Ian Ayris
Will Diamond
S A Tranter
Keith Gingell
Carol Fenlon
Stephen Cooper
Stevin Tasker

Ken McCoy
Gareth Mews
Anthony & Tula Tew
Nick Quantrill
Danny HIll
Roz Goddard
Joe Ridgwell
David Ciurlionis

and introducing

Daniel Mayhew

C000088737

Published by:-

Byker Books
Banbury
Oxon

www.bykerbooks.co.uk

2009

Copyright © retained by individual authors

All rights reserved. No part of this publication may be reproduced, stored in a retrieval system or transmitted in any form or by any means, electronic, mechanical, photocopying recording or otherwise without the permission of the copyright owner.

ISBN 978-0-9560788-3-4

Cover photo by Jonathan Fortune (c) 2009

FANCY ANOTHER?

Well here we are again, it seems only yesterday that we were launching Radgepacket Two with the likes of Sheila Quigley and Ray Banks on a cold day in March and now it's the summer already. We've got some new talent in this issue, authors with acid tongues and razor sharp minds, as well as some compadres of old who have graced our pages with their presence once more.

Inside this here book you'll find stories of vigilantism, giant rats, bent politicians, border reivers (bit of history there for you) and ooh...loads more. We've also blackmailed a couple of established stars of the literary scene into giving us stuff so we don't tell the police where they've buried the bodies - Danny King's back and he's dragged Ken McCoy with him, believe me there's a couple of treats in store there!

Sounds good? Well it doesn't end there kids. We've also got rising star Daniel Mayhew to give us an exclusive piece of his as well as an interview and, in a feat of thievery so good it would impress a politician, we've lifted five signed copies of his top selling book '*Life And How To Live it*' to give away in one of our famous competitions.

As you know this kind of book really is for grown ups, so if you feel you may be offended by the vast amount of profanity, sexual acts and drug references we use in here then you really shouldn't read it.

Mind you, if you're into that then you're gonna love it!

Ed

THOUGHT SO...

Contents

Extras
Featuring Daniel Mayhew

__Keith Gingell__

Keith is a young bloke in an old man's body.
He wishes it was the other way round (don't we
all mate!). After too many years writing fiction
(better known as sales literature) and technical
presentations, he decided to try writing decent fic-
tional literature and poetry. He's been at it (writing that is - steady now!) for about two and a half
years and has had a few poems published.

Big Sid and Hawkeye

At the oil works, they told us we weren't allowed to bring
weapons onto the job anymore. The management stuck
notices up all over the place, telling all three shifts we had a
week to get them off the premises. After that, they said,
they'd do a full search. Anybody found with anything iffy in
their locker would be out the door. Instant dismissal they
called it. They even had union backing. Not that we needed
telling. After what happened to Hawkeye Stevens all the guns
and stuff were back home before any of the notices went up.

I never liked night shifts, especially when the machines were
shut down and it was all quiet. That's when you'd hear 'em.
Rustling and scratching; creeping about above you, then
you'd catch a glimpse of one out the corner of your eye, running along a girder into a dark corner. Sometimes you'd pick
up a sack or move something and there'd be one underneath
and it would run out with a squeak. Scared the living crap
out of me every time.

We all used to carry an iron bar or a lump of galvanised pipe
in the long pocket on the side of our overalls, just in case we
cornered one by accident. Rats make a hell of a noise when
you corner one. Best thing is to whack it before it jumps at
you. I used a broken piston rod from one of the diesel gener-
ators. Found it in a skip outside the engineers' workshop.

For years some guys'd kept catapults in their lockers. They'd
use them to take pot shots at the rats when things were slack.
I tried it, but I'm a useless shot, so I gave mine to my boy.

Most of the blokes fired ball bearings they'd stolen out of the
engineers' stores. But Mad-Mick Donovan brought in a
bloody great bag of marbles he had from when he was a kid.
He had three girls and a vasectomy, so they were no use to
him at home. 'Got a big fucker. Right up the arse, with one of
me tiger's eyes,' he'd say, just about every break time.

Then, Jock McAdams brought in this shooter. An old Webley air pistol he bought at a car-boot for a couple of quid. It wasn't much good, but when he managed to kill a rat with it, things got sort of competitive. Some other guys brought in old air guns they had when they were teenagers.

Joe Barnes and his mate, Hawkeye Stevens, really got the bug. Joe picked up a competition pistol from somewhere - looked like a bloody Luger. So Hawkeye came in with an air rifle. Natch, Joe had to go one better and he bought some Jap thing with a Winchester pump action. So it went on - regular arms race it was. They couldn't bring real guns of course, but those air rifles were bloody lethal. Everybody kept well out of the way when those two went on the hunt.

I don't reckon they killed many rats, despite their fire power. The factory cats were much better at keeping the numbers down. It didn't matter much to me who killed the vermin, so long as they were dead. To me, a rat was a rat ... except for Big Sid that is.

Big Sid was King Rat. The Godfather, we called him. The guys used to tell stories about seeing rats as big as cats on nights, but I never saw any. Most were the size of the ones our tabby dumped on the doorstep most mornings. But Big Sid was different. He was enormous - like a bloody Coypu with ears. Even the feral toms steered clear of Big Sid.

Everybody knew Big Sid. He was very distinctive. Not your normal, grey-brown colour. He had a white flash in his back, a bit like a Nike tick. But it weren't his appearance that was special. He was bloody fearless, even seemed to search us out. He'd sit on a girder or gantry pretending to wash his face - nonchalant like. He'd let you get really near him. Then - whoosh! Gone.

He just turned up one day out of the blue. The guys reckoned he'd escaped from some research lab. Anyhow, it wasn't long before we started seeing little Sids running about with their tell-tale GT stripes. We kind of admired his cheek and pretty much left him alone.

Only Joe and Hawkeye wanted his blood, but they never got close. After a few months Joe was ready to give up, but Hawkeye was obsessed. He hated Big Sid. There was a reason for that. Once, he came face-to-face with him when he was on my shift. Sid just stared at him without moving. The rest of us watched Hawkeye as he squatted down, and crept as close as could: like he was Che-bloody-Guevara or something. He lined up his rifle and took aim. The instant his trigger finger tightened, Sid jumped off the girder and disappeared. Everybody knew it would happen. We pissed ourselves laughing. Everybody except Hawkeye. He took it really hard. Even started staying behind after his shift was finished to hunt Sid down - until the silly bugger forgot to clock out one night. He got a warning for claiming unauthorized overtime. He calmed down after that.

Starting the second weekend of January; it was an annual, three-day maintenance shutdown. We all had Monday off with pay. That was the weekend Hawkeye disappeared. Nobody missed him straight off. His wife was away looking after her mum, who'd just come out of hospital after a stroke. When she got home on Wednesday evening, she assumed Hawkeye was on nights, but when he didn't come home Thursday morning, she started to worry. Before she had a chance to do anything, the shift manager phoned. He told her to remind Hawkeye to get a doctor's certificate if he planned to stay off sick after Thursday, otherwise he'd have his pay docked.

It was another three hours before anybody thought to look for Hawkeye's car in the firm's car-park. If he'd a decent one, instead of a bog-standard Ford Escort, someone might've noticed it before. There were always at least thirty blue Escorts in the car-park day and night. Turned out, Joe

Barnes was the last person to speak to him and it landed him in deep shit. Hawkeye'd asked Joe to clock out for him. He said he'd seen Big Sid at the back of Silo thirteen and wanted to stay behind while it was quiet and get the bastard once and for all. I went all cold when I heard that.

There'd been riots in Lagos, and a big seed crushing plant was torched. Our company got a contract to ship in twenty-thousand tons of Nigerian peanuts for urgent processing. Silo thirteen and nine others were chock full with 'em.

They said one of the security blokes broke down in tears when he saw the walnut stock of Hawkeye's rifle sticking out of the peanuts where it'd fallen in, barrel first. There was no sign of Hawkeye, except for a clean patch in the dust on the walk-way over silo thirteen.

It took two days to remove the auger from under Silo thirteen and clear enough space to get the skips in to collect the peanuts. They'd only filled two when someone saw Hawkeye's legs jam in the outlet. It was a dodgy job getting him out without getting mown down by an avalanche of peanuts.

I didn't see him, but Tom Robbins; the first-aid man - Christ knows what they thought he could do - said he looked very peaceful. He said he looked alright, yet somehow all skewed - flattened like. Not surprising I suppose, considering he'd had the best part of two thousand tons of peanuts sitting on his dome.

Word was, at the autopsy they found every bone in his body was crushed or broken. Apparently he had peanuts in his mouth, stomach, lungs, ears, nose, under his eye-lids even up his jacksy. The sheer weight of them they said. Poor bastard.

The management never allowed silo thirteen to be used again. Nobody went near it after it was de-commissioned.

We didn't see anything of Big Sid and there were no more little Sids. We saw some of his first-born that'd grown up, but they weren't a patch on their father. We assumed Hawkeye'd got him.

Six months later, Bill Mellors, one of the leckies, came into the tea room one morning, looking as white as a sheet. Shaking he was. He'd gone up top to fix a conveyer motor. He'd only seen Big Sid, hadn't he? Sitting on the walk-way over Silo thirteen, looking down into it. Ran off as soon as he saw Bill. It really freaked him out. I left a little while after that. The firm was cutting back and I took redundancy. Got a better job in the new maltings on the harbour. Process operator. Got me own computer terminal and everything. Good money too. But I kept in touch with a couple of old mates. They told me Big Sid would always be seen in the same place: on the walk-way over Silo thirteen, looking inside it ....Weird or what?

Then, about a year ago, I got this call from Mad-Mick. 'Guess what,' he said. 'We found Big Sid dead in the executive car park. One of the cats was dragging his body around and dropped it in a puddle.'

'I'm not surprised, he'd be knocking on a bit,' I said.

'Yeah, but here's the best part. When we examined him, we found two of Hawkeye's air gun pellets lodged right inside his scrotum.'

'That would explain why Big Sid was always up on Silo thirteen,' I said.

'How come?'

'S'obvious, innit? He was looking for his fucking bollocks.'

Will Diamond

Will is from outer-space and currently lives in a
male host who is forty years old. Every night he
sneaks out of his hosts left ear and drinks copious
amounts of lager and whiskey. He is part of the
alien revolution and likes to smoke cigarettes and
eat mint Vienetta. He will be returning to his own
planet soon so read him while you can.

Brian the Bastard

From a very young age I decided that Brian was the ultimate bastard. It all started at the age of five. I was just starting out on my life adventure. Learning to read and write, learning to add and take-away, learning how to make new friends.

Then along came Brian and he ruined my life.

He was a chubby kid who had an almost Mediterranean look. His dark hair hung across his eyes in a left side parting. He was well dressed for those times and had brilliant white teeth and a charming smile. In all honesty I was pleased I had made a friend. If I only knew how our lives would pan out? I would have ran a mile.

*****

By Seventy-Eight punk music ruled the schoolyard and Brian had developed into the biggest boy in the junior school. He ruled the yard with a rod of iron. I would regularly collect in the spoils of his bullying for him and take my thirty percent cut. I didn't like it but in all honesty I was as scared of him as the other kids. We kicked arse all through the summer and we came to the end of term with a pretty good haul to see us through the six-week holidays.

Over the break from school I did what most kids of eleven would do. I camped out, stole milk and veggies and went apple raiding amongst many other things. Brian was my leader and I his trusty aide. But after the summer break things started to go wrong.

*****

We started our senior school the way we had finished off our junior years. Straight in amongst the other kids and establishing control of our age group within two weeks. We were feared immediately, Brian was the muscle and I his clever side kick, always dreaming up ways to obtain things from other kids. Then I came up against a teacher called Mr. Follitt.

You see although Brian was my best mate, he was as thick as a Volvo bumper. We had sort of been forced together. My fear of him and his liking of me were just something that happened. I was always the brain of our outfit and he was the enforcer. So naturally when we went to the senior school we were put in separate classes. To be honest I excelled at school without even trying. Brian however struggled and his problems became more apparent as he grew older.

All the teachers could see what we were doing but they couldn't stop it. We had created a wall of silence, like the Krays. But then two important things happened in the space of one week.

I got called into Mr. Follitt's office for a chat and then I met Gillian Doherty.

Now Mr. Follitt was a decent enough man. You could tell that he was a bit of a hard man. He had that edge about him when he walked across the schoolyard. He was a pretty fair bloke, but he had that mystery about him. I always felt that if I pushed him he would snap. You wouldn't want Mr. Follitt to snap.

So there we were sitting in his office and he says...

'Well Mr. Diamond, you're certainly making an impression in your first year with us. Good or bad I'm not so sure?'

'Thank you sir.' I wasn't so sure either...

'You are top of your English class, doing pretty well in maths, excelling in history and holding your own in geography.

Mr. Singh reports you are doing well in science and Mr. Jonas reports you are a definite for the football team.'

'Well that's all good news sir.'

'So why don't I like you Mr. Diamond?'

There was a long uncomfortable pause.

'Maybe it's beca...'

'Quiet Mr Diamond...I'm getting around to telling you why I don't like you. You see son, you have a pretty good starting point here to go and make a life for yourself. But no...you want to hang around the yard looking tough with your friend O'Connell.'

'But sir...'

'Shut up laddie when I'm talking. Listen to me boy; if you and O'Connell keep these antics up, I will come down on you like a sack of tatties. Now you wouldn't want that...believe me. So I want you to leave this room and think about how you are going to end your ties with Mr. O'Connell. Are we clear on that laddie?'

I nodded my head and looked to the floor as he pushed the door open and watched me leave. I headed for the cloakroom and a dark corner. How was I going to get out of this one? Should I take on Follitt or should I take the risk of upsetting Brian? God only knew. It was around this time that I heard a snivelling sound from the other side of the cloakroom. I walked over to where the sound was coming from and found another first year sitting head bowed and crying.

'What's wrong with you?' I asked in an unsympathetic voice.

'Like you don't know...'

'Well no...actually I don't know.'

'Your friend O'Connell, that's what's wrong.'

She lifted her head to look at me and my feet lifted from the ground and my knees went a bit shaky. It was also around this time that my heart started to beat a little faster and my face turned crimson. I felt like someone had frozen my brain and mouth.

Meet Gillian Doherty.

Long, dark, curly hair and jade green eyes. Thin Irish lips and perfectly straight teeth. She had the start of a bosom and perfect knees. Hallelujah, the heavens opened and the sun shone down into the cloakroom and I got my first meaningful hard on. I fumbled in my trouser pockets to hide the lump at the front of my pants. I sat down on the bench next to her. As expected she shuffled away but she held my stupefied gaze and I'm sure that she gave me a small smile. I sat staring at her like a Guppy; she stopped crying and started to smile. I sort of stopped breathing and felt faint; she started to giggle and looked straight through me with those green eyes of hers.

'Alright arsehole, I see you've met Gill then. She has kindly given us her dinner money for the week. So let's be having you, we'll nip down the shop and get some cigs.'

It was Brian, larger than life and twice as menacing. I slowly stood up and followed him out of the cloakroom. Just as we were leaving I looked back to where Gillian had been sat but she was gone. No wonder. Her knight in shining armour was really a fucking two-bit bully with a big fat bastard for a friend. I followed Brian out of the school gates and down to the corner shop.

We sat on the wall outside of the shop smoking our cigs and

watching the other kids lark about. My heart felt like it would burst, but I just sat, silently thinking about Gillian. Brian was the first to speak.

'I think we should target more girls for money. They put up less resistance.'

'Yeah.'

'I reckon if they're all as easy as Doherty we'll make a packet.'

'Fuck off Brian.'

Brian jumped from the wall and stood facing me. He was shocked at first because I don't think we'd ever had a falling out. Then he started to get angry. His nostrils flared and his eyebrows knitted closer together. I just sat on the wall thinking about Gillian, and about what Mr. Follitt had said. Brian took a step back...

'What do you mean by that Will?'

'Just what I say you fat bastard. I mean fuck off and leave me alone. I've had enough of this shit. I'm sick of picking on people and scaring them. I'm fucking sick of your thick arsed behaviour, I'm sick of having to think for you, I'm sick of your fucking ugly mug you prick.'

I didn't even see the first one coming, but I felt it. I remember falling backwards but the wall somehow kept me up. Brian came lumbering towards me, I quickly sidestepped and gave the fat twat one right in the temple. He fell into the wall and I followed up with a beauty of a right foot into his ribs. I could hear the wind leave his fat fucking lungs at an alarming rate. I grabbed the back of his hair and gave him two full force smacks into the wall. The screams of fight, fight, fight, were now filling my ears. Brian slid to the ground and that was that. I put my hand in his pocket and pulled out two-pound notes and some loose change. I turned to the crowd and walked straight through them with my head held high. I was a hero...

It took me about twenty minutes to locate Gillian. She was standing with Becky Smith over by the netball courts. She said something to her friend as I approached and Becky picked up her bag and left. I'm not going to bore you with the details. Let's just say that from the minute I pushed those two crisp one pound notes into Gillian's hand we were an item.

I felt her hand wrap around mine as she leant in close and we set off across the schoolyard. Everyone was staring at us; you could hear the low whispered voices without ever catching what they were actually saying. As we turned towards the science block there was a commotion behind us. I let go of Gillian's hand and spun round to see what was happening.

That's when Brian's big chunky fist caught me square on the jaw. Hero to zero in approximately one second. I don't really remember anything else apart from waking up in the first aid room with Mr Follitt standing over me.

'Well done Diamond laddie, you did yourself proud.'

Brian was expelled from the school a day later and things went back to normal. Gillian and I were still an item and I had gained the respect of my fellow pupils. Life looked like it was going to be good, how wrong could I be?

For the next four years every time I crossed paths with Brian O'Connell there was fireworks. I'll be the first to admit that he won most of our encounters, but I had my moments. The thing that bothered me the most was that they seemed to be getting increasingly violent. Brian had formed quite a reputation for himself. He had also made some very dodgy acquaintances along the way. I was being forced into an impossible situation. The older we grew the more at risk I was becoming. At the age of eighteen things were looking really bad. Brian was making my life hell and I was afraid he was going to eventually finish me off.

Then I got a lifeline...

Brian discovered the joys of drugs. I'll hold my hands up here, so did I. But while Gillian and I were travelling the country getting off our faces on ecstasy, Brian was bombing speed like it was going out of fashion and sitting in filthy houses smoking resin. As you may have guessed already, he graduated to heroine and I went down the path of cocaine.

Neither is a good choice, but while I became a well dressed young man with a beautiful girlfriend. Brian became a skinny, spotty bastard who seemed to owe the whole world money. Brian O'Connell was dead and buried as far as I was concerned. Our hatred faded and I even gave him money once. I just couldn't bear to have him talk to me so I shoved twenty in his hand and walked away.

My life took a turn for the better and his for the worse.

*****

I pretty much sailed through the next fifteen years of my life. I had the nice house, the nice car and Gillian and I were as strong as ever. We now had two children and life was good. I still went out to town with a few of the lads I had known from school and I was saving to buy a villa in Italy.

Then, one Friday night, I was sitting in the Black Swan when Dave, one of my oldest friends, burst through the door with blood all over his head. He fell to his knees, and then to the floor as a woman in the bar screamed. I rushed over to him and tried to get some sense out of him.

'Dave, Dave, fucking hell man what happened?'

He looked up at me and held my arms with trembling hands. Half of his ear was missing and his nose was well done in.

'It's that bastard O'Connell, he's back with a vengeance and he's looking for you Will.'

To say my arse dropped out would be an understatement. Every haunting memory of Brian came flooding back. I felt like spewing my guts there and then. My mobile phone rang and an unknown number showed on the screen. I slid the slider to open and answered.

'Aye?'

'Ah just the man...Hello old friend it's Brian O'Connell. Just to let you know that I bumped into one of your old pals today and gave him a message for you. I always liked Dave, shame I had to bite his ear off...Anyway, just to let you know that you're a lucky man to have a wife like Gillian...She hasn't changed a bit.'

'You fucking stay away from her you cunt. I'm fucking warning you. You go near her and I'll do fucking time for you.'

The phone just went dead.

After I had made sure Gillian and the kids were safe I made a couple of calls to friends. Two of those friends sat in my dining room discussing what to do about O'Connell. First up they said I needed to guarantee my family's safety and second up there was going to have to be some pay back for what happened to Dave. I thought it better to be proactive on this one; I couldn't wait around for O'Connell to come to me.

So that brings me to the present.

I'm sitting on an old washing machine in Dave's garage. Dave is also here, along with Mike and Jeff two of our closest friends. We are staring into a hole in his garage floor. It's roughly seven-foot in length by about five across the width. I'd say we got to a depth of about nine feet and it was bloody hard work.

Everyone is surprisingly upbeat about tonight's task. We've already sunk a few tins of Stella and there's still another full case to go. Mike is patrolling the perimeter of the hole. I keep thinking he's going to jump in and try it for size. Jeff keeps shuddering, I'm not sure if it's the cold air or the thought of what's going on that is making him shake. Dave looks quite smug...payback time. I'm feeling a bit numb to be honest but like I said the atmosphere is still a good one. Everyone seems to be waiting for someone else to make the first move.

O'Connell breaks the silence as his piss pools on to the floor at his feet. We all turn to face him. He's taped to an old chair that Dave stands on to paint his ceilings. His brow has deep furrows across it and the perspiration from his body has soaked his blue cotton T-shirt. His stonewashed blue jeans are soaked at the crotch area and down his left leg. A puddle is growing on the garage floor as he mouths something from beneath the strip of tape across his mouth.

He didn't really give me much choice. He posted a letter through my door telling me that he would kill my first-born and nail the other bastard to a tree. He also mentioned a few ideas he had lined up for Gillian. That was probably his downfall. Before the letter we were considering giving him a good hiding and taking our chances...but now...well...he knew what was coming. I walked behind him and picked up the weighted baseball bat that was leaning against the wall. I moved back around the chair so I was facing him. I set my feet square on to him and raised the bat to shoulder height.

'Take the fucking tape off.'

Dave leant in from the side and tore the tape away from his mouth.

O'Connell looked deep into my eyes...I slowly swung the bat to my right-hand side

'Wanker...'

*****

Dave sliced through the tape holding O'Connell to the chair with a Stanley knife. Then between us we dragged him to the floor and laid him next to the hole. Jeff passed another round of drinks to each of us and one by one we opened the cans. I gulped at mine and drank three-quarters in one go. Then I knelt on the ground and rolled the unconscious O'Connell into the hole. I swear I saw his eyes open as the first shovel full of soil and brick landed on his chest. Maybe it was just my mind playing tricks on me? Maybe it was the thought that he might regain consciousness before he suffocated? Maybe I wanted him to?

After a couple of hours the hole was filled and Dave was mix-ing some concrete to flush it over. I grabbed another can and turned to look at the friends who had helped me. Friends, who like me, would carry this secret for the rest of their lives. I raised my can into the air.

'Rest in peace Brian the Bastard...and we'll see you in Hell.'

<u>Danny Hill</u>

Danny's been writing since he could hold a
pen in his hand and has been published in various places. Over the past couple of years he's been
collaborating with others in a regeneration arts
project in his native Stoke-on-Trent. He is currently working on his first novel, with more twists,
he explains, than Peaches Geldof's knickers after a
night in China White.

Past Glories

I'm awoken by the pale half-light that seeps through the
cracks in John's thick bedroom curtains. This is the part of
my weekend I invariably despise the most. Sunday mornings.
Every week, it seems, leaving him is becoming more and
more difficult.

Pushing myself into a sitting position from John's tatty,
worn, yet oh-so-comfortable double bed, I crane my neck
around to check the time on the LCD display. 07:01. Not that
I need such added confirmation. I always wake a few minutes
before he does. And any minute now, he will wake up, turn
over to face me and say the words I have become so accustomed to hearing yet find it increasingly difficult to close my
ears to.

'Don't go. Stay. Please stay.' John's words would be spoken
like a hushed mantra, his eyes like dark pools of anticipation,
probing mine for reciprocation.

I rub the grit from my eyes and they soon adjust to the dim
tableau of John's bedroom. He isn't a tidy man. Self-preser-
vation, too, is not his sharpest suit. Dirty clothes and underwear are strewn across the threadbare carpet like vast puddles of cotton and denim. The furniture in the room is circa-
1970's, all cheap pine-imitation wardrobes and bedside cabi-
nets, ageing floral-patterned wallpaper peeling from the crest
of the wall with polystyrene alcove missing from the corners.
A few weeks ago I risked a glance under his bed and immediately wished I hadn't; the evidence of too many ready-meals
in bed and his profound lack of culinary skills lay there like a
killer's bloodied armoury. But John's only crime is his
slovenliness. His weakness is me.

Last night, before John went to sleep, he wept. This had been
nothing new, I know. His tears have become as habitual as
my visits here. The reason for his tears were because we had,

again, failed to make love. He told me that he regarded himself as a failure, somebody that could never do anything
right. I remember thinking just how low a man's self-esteem
can get. John, it seemed, had hit the bottom a long time ago.
I tried to assure him, telling him that he had had lots to
drink, it happens to all men. This seemed to placate him, as
he settled into my arms, curled up a ball, his thick, warm
tears meandering down my chest, between my breasts and on
to the sheets. Minutes later, he was asleep. It didn't take
long. It never did.

Sitting upright in bed, naked, I imagine how I must look to
the world right now. Old. Old and tired. My roots are showing at the base of my peroxide blonde hair and my make-up
is smudged beyond recognition. I know this without the benefit of a mirror. I reach into my bag and withdraw a brush,
drag it across my scalp so as to tie my hair back. I notice that
my breasts aren't what they once were - firm and pointed;
now they hang as large weights, the content unsubstantiated
by the aged skin that supported them so well in my youth.

John's snoring is but a gentle rumbling. I turn my head to
where the sound is emanating from and stare at his naked
back, thick with dark bristles; motionless, save for the occa-
sional swelling and deflating of his breathing. He could certainly do with some exercise, I think, staring at the fleshy
rubber band around his waist. John was also one of those
men that has the misfortune to believe that a few strands of
wispy hair combed over their scalp was enough to camou-
flage their premature baldness. But then, I remember, it
wasn't John's looks that attracted me to him that evening
when we first met.

After work my colleagues and I favour a late-night drinking
bar in the middle of Stoke town centre - Harry's bar, situated
directly opposite the mass of impressive architecture that is
St Philips' church. Given its late licence, the venue is patron-
ised mainly by serious drinkers and students, with

Staffordshire University being a ten minute walk away.
There's always a buzz in the place, always something on,
more often than not featuring bands or DJs from the area.

 When I spotted John, however, sitting alone at the bar, he
seemed impervious to the euphoria all around him, his solitude characterised by the way he sat slumped over his pint,
gazing absentmindedly into its contents. I suppose it was
born out of a sense of pity that I decided to join him, taking a
stool next to him. I don't like to see people alone, and it's one
of my many foibles that I am more than able to strike conversation with almost anybody that I have never met before. At
first, though, prising a sentence out of John, if you'll excuse
the cliché, was like trying to draw blood from a stone. He
seemed happy in his solitude, and my animated and rambling attempts to draw him into conversation were met by
aloof nods and noncommittal shrugs, and answered by droning monosyllables. And just when I was about to give up on
him, perched on my stool to leave, he grabbed my wrist.

'Don't go. Please stay,' he whispered, almost tentatively. That
was the first time I looked into his eyes. His eyes had a
watery, weakened look; I read from them a map of a thousand emotional journeys you wouldn't want to take, a score
of heartaches, trials and tribulations, a lifetime of self-pity.
He had the kindest eyes I have ever seen. I told him that I
wasn't going anywhere. Not yet. He smiled softly then, extri-
cated himself from his vice-like grip on my wrist and gently
apologised.

John's story was nothing new. Nothing I hadn't heard before.
He had been married for twenty-four years, he explained,
had two children who had since flown the nest, developed
careers, children and lives of their own. His face was etched
into a beaten expression as he went to say that his wife had
left not long after. Whether his wife's disposition was due to
another man, I do not know, but I can guess; the pain in his
eyes bade me not to probe any further.

I felt a gratuitous urge to grab him by his collar and scream at him. Wake yourself up, man! Snap out of it. But I didn't. Of course not. Instead I saw John as a challenge I must overcome, to somehow teach him to relinquish the impregnable cloak of self-pity that shrouded his confidence and his sense of self. As the night wore on, I did as I promised him. As I kept his company I endeavoured to make him laugh in my magnanimous, rambling way, drawing observations and anecdotes from my life's experiences, indulging him. I wanted to make him forget, even if just for a while, his troubles. We carried on like that all night; laughing, joking, with a subtext of mild flirtation. When the night was over and the bar staff were clearing out, he told me hadn't had so much fun since God-knows-when (his own words). I agreed. John has this endearing way of holding my hand and simultaneously circling his thumb over the top of my palm. It was while he was doing this that he asked me to come back to his house. He told me that I was beautiful. I nearly laughed. Perhaps I would've done had anybody else told me so, but I respected John too much to ridicule him. And I believed him. So, illustrating my obligations to him beforehand, I agreed to go back with him.

John seemed slightly embarrassed on arriving home to his two-up two-down in Fenton, given the mess scattered around the place. The kitchen uncharacteristically and surprisingly clean. This, I deduced, was probably because John hadn't used his cooker since his wife had left, probably couldn't cook beans on toast if he tried, instead living off take-aways and microwave meals. We talked for a bit in his living room, then John and I went up to his bedroom. What the subsequent sex lacked in duration, it more than made up for in passion. John held me for hours afterwards, stroking my hair, telling me how beautiful I was. At this point I suppose I was already adapting to his foibles; the constant flattery that often surpasses itself through repetition and gradually enters that grey area between being overbearing and uncomfortable for the recipient. John spent a long time simply lying in bed and looking into my eyes. Ashamedly, it was often me that broke contact. Because, perhaps, in John's pained, brown eyes I saw a reflection of myself. It has been a long time since I have felt strongly about a man. Oh yes, John isn't the only one out of the two of us that has been hurt. But I wasn't going to tell him that.

In the weeks that followed he insisted that we went out together, before invariably ending up back at his house. He is such an old romantic, taking me out for meals, dancing and, once, to the cinema in Festival Park. He made me feel like a teenager again, but it was because of this the inevitable sense of embarrassment I felt, that people our age shouldn't be going to the cinema, would not abate. I explained this to John, but the childlike enthusiasm he displayed in "courting" me seemed to blind him from the reality of the situation. Perhaps it was me. In endeavouring to teach John to live again, I was simply compounding the problems I already had. Perhaps I was the one that needed to drop my guard. Reluctantly, I stopped our little dates, but I still agreed to visit him at his home at weekly intervals for sex. John seemed crestfallen after I had said this, and produced two tickets for a football match he had purchased for the following Saturday from his wallet. Seeing the hangdog expression on his face I was becoming so familiar with, I agreed to go. Just this once.

Now, admittedly, football isn't really my thing. For me, the way I've always seen it, is that men and football go together. With this in mind, I surprised myself when we arrived at the Britannia Stadium at how many women and children were in attendance. Football has changed since I last went to a match. The boredom, however, of standing still for almost two hours watching a pig-skin flying from one end of the pitch to another, hadn't. When I saw the change in John though, it surprised me. For those ninety minutes of football, John had become instantly animated, gesticulating wildly and shouting encouragement to the players. He would occasionally turn his head to check on me, sitting silently filing my nails, to ask me if I was enjoying the game, before furtively checking back to the game, seeing some minor injustice occur and stridently abusing the referee. I had no idea he could be so vocal. His podgy, unshaven face carried a flush from his neck to his brow from the exertion of shouting so loudly. I had always thought of him as the type of football fan who studied the game studiously and monosyllabically. It just shows how well you think you know someone.

Outside the ground we ate burgers and John voiced his contempt for the current Stoke City manager to anyone that was in earshot. All around us were murmured nods of acquiescence from people or families hurrying to beat the traffic and get home. As we made our way to the pub, I felt the burger turn to acid in my stomach and complained about the pain in my feet. I only wish I'd had the foresight not to wear heels. Immediately John, like the gentleman he is, with a slight smile, offered to give me a piggy-back to the pub. I slapped him playfully and told him to grow up.

The pub was already packed-out, even though the game had just finished. The bar-staff struggled to cope with the demand, with impatient customers five or six deep along the length of the bar. I decided to take a seat in the corner and wait for John. I sat down beneath a large window and scanned the tableau in the bar. Red and white replica shirts was the homogenous fashion of the day, with some of the men's guts and man-boobs swaying precariously under the thin material as they balanced their pints walking from the bar. A group of people were standing in the centre of the pub, looking up at a host of television screens suspended from the panelled ceiling, spread out like a mural along a bricked stanchion; people presumably looking out for league positions and rival teams' results from the final score-boards. To my left a group of middle-age men were in deep conversation, huddled around their table to drown out the noise in the pub.

One older man broke out into a large cackle at their shared
joke. A flustered-looking glass collector removed several dirty
glasses from my table, stacking them almost as tall as she
was.

John arrived back smiling with his pint and my gin and
tonic. A voice from the table to our left recognised him and
we joined a group of men of a similar age to John. In fact,
any one of them could have been a carbon copy of him. He
introduced me as his girlfriend and I felt my neck reddening
slightly. Again, I felt we had crossed a bridge somewhere that
could inevitably lead to my embarrassment on the other side.
Luckily, his friends didn't seem to notice how bashful I was
at John's remark. In fact, they barely registered my profile at
all. Like I say... football, a boys' playground.

Within seconds John was emerged in deep conversation with
his friends, occasionally craning his head around to smile at
me. His smile asked, Are you okay? My return smile was spoken as an affirmative. It wasn't as though I was deliberately
avoiding conversation that day (I'm very far from being
socially introverted) but when the topics follow one prescrip-
tion (football) and one's knowledge is slightly lacking to say
the least, a third-person perspective is probably the best
stance to take. Besides, I enjoyed watching John tossing his
own morsels into the conversational salad, regaling his
friends with the various footballing anecdotes he had accu-
mulated through the years. He seemed to be enjoying himself, so animated and enthusiastic in his reminiscence, his
eyes flickering elatedly like shards of ice. His genuine excite-
ment was contagious. It occurred to me that John and his
friends took these nostalgic journeys every home game, to
relive these past glories they spoke so fondly of. They spoke
of goals, games and players from the 1972 cup-winning team;
players, they collectively illustrated, that would eat these
modern-day, overpaid fancy-Dans for breakfast. I told them
that I could remember the team returning home from
Wembley on an open-top bus. A sea of red and white.

It was as though the whole city had come to a standstill. You literally couldn't move for cheering people that day. John's friends seemed pleased with these observations of mine. But most of all, John seemed pleased with me, smiling and holding my hand, and that was all that mattered.

The LCD display now says 07:19. I dress quietly, so as not to wake him, even though I know it will be seconds before he wakes anyway. Like I say, there has been no room for alteration in our short relationship, and it won't start here. I see John's arm reach over his side and fill the hollow I have since vacated. He searches there and turns over to face me. His eyes flash with discernment and quiet alarm when he realises I am almost ready to leave.

'Don't go. Stay. Please stay,' he whispers, rubbing the grit from his eyes.

Sometimes I feel as though I am falling in love with John, but, deep down, I know that just is not the case. John and I aren't so different, I realise that now. The only difference being that the fact that John has been married for so long has brought him codependency. In finding John I have suddenly come to terms with how lonely I am. And I have been lonely for considerably longer than he has. I have become accustomed to it, no matter how hard I try to convince myself otherwise. And no matter how hard I try to fight it, there is an area at the back of my brain that nags me to make a go of things with John.

But I can't. I couldn't do that to myself, and especially not to someone as kind as John.

I don't love him. Not really. It would be unprofessional of me otherwise. I illustrated my obligations to him before I agreed to return to his house with him that night. My conscience is clear. It's business, that's all it is.

'I can't, John. You know I can't.' John's resigned eyes rest into the lilac sheets beneath him. I pocket the wad of folded notes on the bedside cabinet and count them. One hundred and fifty pounds. Not bad for a night's work, and certainly not bad for an old girl like me.

'Same time next week?' I ask. I think I see his head nod vaguely, but it's difficult to be sure.

As I leave I kiss him on the cheek. I wonder how long I can keep doing this. Each week, it seems, leaving him becomes more and more difficult.

Ian Ayris

Ian hears voices. Sweary naughty voices.
Telling him tales of silly things and violence.
Instead of seeking psychiatric help, he writes
these stories down and sends them to Byker
Books. Surviving on Pot Noodles alone he awaits
sectioning by the relevant authorities, aware that
his lifelong support of Dagenham & Redbridge
merely strengthens the case against him.

The Rise and Demise of Fat Kenny

Fat Kenny was an arsehole. No-one ever doubted that. Not even his own mum. I remember in the Bell and Bucket one time, Bethnal Green, Kenny starts giving it the biggun, getting all intimidating like, just 'cos some kid's bumped his pint. Next thing, his Mum comes over, grabs him by the ear and twists it hard as you like. She kept twisting 'til he apologised to the kid for scaring the shit out of him. Kenny was almost in tears at the end. So was we, it was fuckin' hilarious. He was forty-one at the time.

Now Kenny had his fingers in a lot of pies but there are some pies not even a fat bastard like him should touch. Yeah, Fat Kenny was a proper arsehole, but what become of him, well, it was a crying shame. That's what it was. A bleedin' crying shame. We all knew he was running a couple of brasses out of a flat in Tilbury and that he dabbled in a bit of puff. He could get hold of an 'alf decent pair of trainers if you wanted, knocked-off aftershave, bit of jewellery, stuff like that. Strictly small time. Back end of last year, everything changed.

We was in the boozer, Sad Keith, Tommo and me, when the door bangs open and in strides Fat Kenny. Now, Kenny was never a strider. He was more of a shuffler, like the rest of us, always had been, but this night he strides in like he owns the whole fuckin' world. Gone was the oversized, Chinky-stained t-shirt and gone was the arse hanging out of his jeans. All suited up in Italian clobber, he was. My old man was in the rag trade all his life, so I knows top clobber when I sees it. Fuckin' Brioni suit - three grand a pop. Black cashmere overcoat hanging off his shoulders, silk scarf round his neck. Looked like he just walked off The Sopranos. Sad Keith spits out his beer, Tommo's fag falls out and I nearly chokes on me pork scratchings. Then Kenny up and buys a round for the whole fuckin' place. It was like he'd gone all big time overnight. Fucking unbelievable.

A couple of hours later, he squeezes up to me at the bar smelling of aftershave and hair cream. For the last ten years he'd smelled of nothing but chips and piss. Aftershave and fuckin' hair cream, for fucks sake.

'You all right, Kenny?' I says, 'Had a touch on the gee gees?'

He smiles at me, sort of conspiratorial, like. Doesn't say a word.

'So, what's up, Kenny, what's with all the clobber?'

Kenny tries to tap his nose and misses. He's a bit pissed by now. For a fat bastard, he never could hold his drink.

'Come 'ere,' he slurs, pulling me closer, 'I'll tell you a little secret.'

They're not really the words I ever want to hear from a grown man but my curiosity gets the better of me, and I lean in.

'You won't tell no-one, will you?' he says.

'No, Kenny,' I says, 'course not.'

'Good boy.'

Then he tells me how his brother's mate, Ronnie Swordfish, a well known face on the manor and one horrible cunt, taps him up one day and asks him to do a little job. Kenny's given a pile of cash and told to put a certain amount on a certain dog at half a dozen different bookies. I suspect its a blood doping scam 'cos the odds are always as long as your arm, but it's clear Kenny's fuckin' clueless. He's happy just to be mixing it with the big boys.

All over town, there's probably twenty five other desperate looking fuckers, hand picked for the job, doing exactly the same as Kenny. They put on just enough to keep the odds long, collect the winnings, act like they can't believe their luck, then hand it all over to the big man. Each time a different dog, different track, different bookies. Four or five races a week and Ronnie Swordfish has got cash coming out his arse. Kenny and the others get their cut, and everyone's a winner.

'So what's the next dog?' I ask Kenny, half joking, not really expecting nothing.

He puts down his pint and looks me straight in the eye, really serious, like.

'You're me mate, John, ain't you?'

'Yeah, course, Kenny. We go back a long way, you and me.'

He's got tears in his eyes.

Kenny was the lad we never picked for football, but who stayed to watch anyway. Who'd turn up on my doorstep, out the blue, asking me mum if I could come out and play. I'd tell her I was doing my homework, or something. It weren't just me, I'd see him knock up and down the whole street. One door after another, shut in his face. In the end, no-one bothered to even open the door to him. Poor bastard. His dad used to beat the shit out of him for being fat. So did we.

Kenny puts his hand on me shoulder, looks at me hard, as if he's really sizing me up. Then he whispers, 'Biscuit Boy second race, Walthamstow this Friday. Put your fuckin' house on it.'

'Cheers, Kenny.' I say, and he gives me a big hug and heads for the shithouse.

Friday night comes round, and me and Tommo and Sad Keith are stood at the dog track freezing our bollocks off.

I had to tell 'em. They was me mates. I decided not to put my house on it like Kenny said. The council would never have stood for that. In the end, I put on a monkey - everything I had, and Keith and Tommo a long'un each. Thought we was the only ones in the know but when the odds start falling from sevens to nigh on evens, I know something's up. And when that dog comes flying round the corner like Linford fuckin' Christie, and half the fuckin' crowd's on it's feet, I know Kenny's fucked up. We made a packet. So did every other fucker Kenny told. Stupid bastard.

The pub had a lock-in that night, in honour of Fat Kenny. Everyone was shaking his hand, slapping his back, the birds was all over him. See, a lot of us are pretty strapped, just make ends meet, sad to say, you know. Kenny helped us all out. He done us all a favour. Kills me to think of what we did to him as a kid. He grew up a right lump. Soft as shit, mind, if you knew him. But he had a chip on his shoulder, Kenny. You saw it in his eyes. Yeah, we still took the piss out of him, but we never pushed it.

I sees Tony behind the bar hand Kenny the phone. Couldn't been a few seconds before Kenny hands it back. I make out to Keith and Tommo I need a piss, just to get wind of what's going down. I sense it's not good. I gets to the other side of the bar from Kenny, catch his eye, and see he's back on the phone. Place is packed and some fucker pushes in front of me, blocks my view. When I get past, I can't see Kenny nowhere. I ask Tony. He just says, 'Business'.

They pulled Kenny out the Thames a couple of days later. Some old girl with her dog says she see him walking down the steps to the water and that he just kept on going. She said it was like the river just swallowed him up.

A few days after Kenny was found, Ronnie Swordfish and a dozen of his knuckle-draggers get hauled in by the Old Bill. Anonymous tip-off, apparently.

With the form he's got, he won't be seeing the light of day for the rest of his fuckin' life.

Funny, you never know what festers inside a man, just laying there, waiting. It took a lot of bollocks to do what Kenny did. A lot of bollocks. The way I sees it, that last night in the pub, it weren't gonna get no better for him. Rather than face Ronnie Swordfish and his apes, he'd decided to call it a day. Go out with his head held high and a fuckin' smile on his face and he made sure he took Ronnie Swordfish with him.

Yeah, Fat Kenny was an arsehole. No-one ever doubted that. But he was our arsehole, and I miss him. We all do.

Stevin Tasker

Stevin is a Geordie scribe working through
that difficult second novel. He drifted off one
day and looked up the lawless and truly violent
Northern borderlands of days gone by. This led
him to pen the following story. He plans to do
some proper research and turn it into a series of
best selling novels. On an unrelated note his
favourite food is beans on toast.

The Reiver

The rider stood high in the saddle. He strained his eyes trying to see across the wide valley floor stretching out beneath his horse's hooves. He waited alone, here at dusk on the hillside. He watched as the morning mist rolled away across the ground. His glare unwavering, as if he could see through the peat walls of the smallholding nestled at the cross roads near the base of the valley. He cast his eyes over to the cattle taking advantage of the good grazing nearby and watched the two riders dismount and enter the building. He waited in the safety of the mist as the third rider came from the west riding the white horse. By then he'd seen enough. The old Smithy had told it right. The three were in it together. The fierce wind battered his face but made no such impression on the wet heather that covered the valley. Rain peppered his steel bonnet and he pulled his damp riding cloak across his tunic. He'd seen worse weather abroad these past few years. After what seemed an age he finally turned his horse away and set off back down the old shepherd track behind him. His brow heavily furrowed as he resided his weary head to the fact that he must kill three men.

'Did you see them?' The smithy enquired as if to seek acceptance in the truth he had told. The hot steam rising from the forge behind him.

'I did. I thank you for your trouble.' Jack was thankful that this old smith seemed less inclined to ask more questions about his business. Jack glanced at the horse behind him.

'See to the hobbler there will you.'

'Aye,' The blacksmith walked off towards the sturdy horse standing at his gate.

Jack made his way to the small room above the smithy. He

stretched out on the soft straw bedding above the workshop. The furnace beneath him ensured his warmth despite the howling wind outside. The small town he'd come back to hadn't changed much this last few years. A lawless border between England and Scotland ruled over by whichever families were strongest at the time.

He'd left this place for the mercenary life nearly three years since and had seen heavy fighting in France and Ireland in the pay of the highest bidder. His return had brought him to his father's Pele house in the West March where he found it sitting in ruins after being burned to the ground. Not a single thing left, no cattle and his father gone presumed by those around to be dead. It was common knowledge of course. The Grahams' had come Reiving from East March; they'd taken the cattle and what they could carry and had put the dwelling to the torch. Border law dictated that the Hot Trod, the right to take back one's property by force if necessary, could be carried out but the lawful time for that had passed. The March warden and his men had turned a blind eye but common knowledge told it that the two Graham brothers and Hobie Maxwell were the ones responsible for entering the house.

He lay still on his back as the thoughts invaded his mind once more. His Father, the cattle and the home he once knew were nothing short of memories now in his adult years. Reiving operated within Border Law; it was something he knew plenty about having been brought up with it since a child. He didn't want their cattle, their possessions and nor did he want to raze their children's home to the ground; he would take retribution for his father though and it would be dreadful. Bloody and dreadful.

Although his limbs were well rested they still groaned when he rose and stretched. The scars of battle were visible on his naked torso; he was long past caring about the toll his profession had taken on him. A pike stab here a sword slash there, not to mention many a troubled night. He pulled a tunic over his broad shoulders and then a quilted cloth jak of plaite; its small overlapping pieces of metal providing his light armour. He'd served in the company of decent men and good soldiers but when the time came to leave he knew it. He'd taken his spoils and come back home to make a life for himself.

He rode that night, using the cover of the darkness and his recollection of the Reivers paths between the bleak rolling hills. The winding cross roads cut into the earth between the villages and settlements would take him back to the shepherds' path where he'd been earlier that day. There he would wait. He didn't wait long. The three men he was looking for left the homestead, two eastward, the other, on the white horse, took the path to the west. Better odds tonight he thought. He turned towards the west path at a gallop.

He met Hugh Graham on the shepherds' path between the small homestead and the first village inside West March. He'd positioned himself in full view; his horse took up the width of the path. He looked directly at his quarry as he slowed to a trot some twenty feet away.

Hugh Graham steadied his steed at a comfortable distance. 'Move aside rider. I've urgent business up this path.'

'I've urgent business with you Hugh Graham.'

'Thinking to run me through are you?' His grinding baritone thundered the distance between the two men, the overbearing confidence of a braggart and a bully seeping out with each word.

'Aye. I've come to run you through.'

The rider urged his mount to charge along the track. Nostrils flared and muscles stretched as powerful hooves chopped up muddy ground. He quickly unsheathed his lance and was upon his quarry before Graham could muster a plan of his own. The lance struck Graham in the shoulder; he tumbled backwards falling roughly to the ground. The rider turned with the lay of the land, his horse made easy work of the worn path. He quickly dismounted but Hugh was already on his feet. Shaken but ready and with a heavy English blade in his hands.

They circled each other; murderous intent abound and caution a distant watcher. They smashed at one another with their swords. Heavy footfalls on wet ground did little to calm the animal aggression. Jack kept cutting and slashing until he wore his opponent down. His practised sword arm accompanied by sweeping arcs from the dagger in his left hand.

Cut and thrust and move. It had seen him through many a battle. Cut, thrust, move. Time and again he kept at it; finally, the sword found its home. He drew a heavy breath as he pierced the man's stomach. Thrusting again and again he drove the blade home. He followed up by stabbing with the dagger. The final life breath seeped from his quarry causing a plume of smoke to rise in the damp air as his lifeless body slumped to the ground. Jack stood for a time. Just breathing in the cool air as sweat glistened on his forehead. With blood on both blades he stood still as the thrill of battle slowly melted away. His body heaved beneath his light armour and his steel bonnet became heavy once more. He sheathed his sword and released the leather helmet strap to expose his cropped brown hair to the cool breeze.

Back at the smithy he paid for his lodgings and the care of his horse or hobbler as he referred to it. The smithy agreed to find a discreet buyer for the horse and pack Jack had newly acquired. If he recognised the horse he didn't seem to show it. It would be a day or so before Hugh Graham would be missed and then only by his two confederates. Jack had made sure that the body would never be found so for now he could fill his belly with food and ale. He had coins enough to live well but after the discovery of his father's home he'd decided to remain discreet. He had left most of his belongings with the Monks at Tynemouth having served with one of their number before the man took to the cloth.

The tavern was awash with Brawlers, Reivers, Whores and Mercenaries. Some of the Warden's men were in there too. They each cast a weary eye to his sword arm as he crossed the room towards them.

'Warden,' Jack nodded politely as he crossed behind the fat drunkard and stepped towards a table at the back of the room. The Warden could barely raise his head. Jack didn't know him but he knew his type. Nothing but a lapdog to the highest paying family.

'That's a handsome dirk you have there.' The weedy man to Warden's right hand piped up.

'What of it?' Jack turned sharply.

'Nothing, nothing,' The man shrunk towards the table.

Jack realised it had been a mistake to hang Hugh Graham's dagger from his belt. No matter. What's done is done. Smithy told it that the food was decent here and the ale strong. Just what he needed; a plate of lamb and a flagon of strong ale. Afterwards he took to the upstairs with a 'lady' by the name of Beth. It had been a long time since he felt a smooth hand on his body and by his reckoning he needed that as well.

Rested and well fed he rode out again the next night. He didn't have to wait long. He kept inside the tree line as the rider came near. He thanked his luck that the Eastward path was peppered by many a secluded copse of trees. Another night ride along the forgotten paths had brought Jack to his ambush point. He'd prepared the road before him with large bracken and bramble bushes torn from the trees around him.

The rider approached at a steady pace but slowed as he drew near. The sloping valley wall beside him and the tree line to his left gave him cause for concern. His right hand slipped from the reins before releasing the small crossbow by his side. The horse padded gently forward as he surveyed the terrain before him. Listening, watching in the failing light. The well fed mount beneath him snorted and shook its heavy head as if anxious to maintain a steady pace.

Jack raced from the trees with the pike staff raised high. He'd misjudged the distance badly and the rider had ample time to raise and fire the deadly arrow. It flew high but true, catching Jack in the shoulder.

'Agghh,' he howled in pain as the bolt cut through his light armour. His arm dropped but he still charged forward managing to stab the pike end deep into the rider's thigh. The rider's cotton britches offered no protection and he screamed as the pike tore into his flesh. He smashed the crossbow down on the pike shaft. It fell to the soft ground below.

In a desperate attempt to make some gain in the fight Jack grappled for the rider's foot. The mounted man twisted and turned, at the same time trying to unsheath his sword. Jack's hands slipped on the wet boot. The horse bucked and stumbled as if unhappy at being jostled, finally it reared skyward and the rider fell to the ground. Jack quickly unsheathed his rapier. The burning pain of the bolt in his shoulder heightened his senses and his grasp on the leather bound handle felt strong. He stepped around the horse to look at its rider; he writhed there on the wet ground, one hand clutching the deep wound on his thigh, the other struggling to unsheathe the sword that had fallen beneath his outstretched body.

Jack stepped closer.

'I've business with you William Graham. You owe me a life.'

'Mercy, mercy, a life? I've not killed a man.'

'The Pele House at West March. You and Maxwell put it to flame.'

'Aye, ah threw the torches but I didn't kill the man. That was Hobie Maxwell.'

'Where did you bury the man?'

'Bury him?' A momentary lapse allowed Will Graham a snort.

Jack dug the tip of his blade into the man's throat. 'Tell me where you buried him and I might let you live,'

'We didn't bury him.' He paused seemingly resigned to his fate. 'We burned him along with his house.'

Jack took in the words as he stood over the pitiful sight. The man's face contorted as he begged for mercy; he pleaded with Jack to put away the sword. He offered all he had and more but Jack had stopped listening. He couldn't hear the words any longer, nor did he hear the gurgling cough as he leant on the sword handle, pushing it deeper into the man's throat.

He managed to tether the second horse to his own. He hoped the knot would hold but didn't have the strength to tie it any tighter. He hauled his body onto the horse and winced when he fully realised the pain he was in. Sitting heavy in the saddle he took hold of the reins. The searing pain in his shoulder seemed to intensify with every clack of the hooves beneath him. With the Smithy in sight he slumped nearer to the mane floating in front of him and managed to ride to within crawling distance of the now familiar shack.

All he remembered before being consumed by cold blackness was getting a face full of dirt as he slumped to the ground.

'Mmph' Jack mumbled

'You'll do well to do keep quiet while I pull this out,'

'Aggghh,' He almost bit clean through the leather strap
jammed into his mouth.

Beth quickly tore the small arrow from his shoulder. He
slumped back down to the straw and passed out again.

He awoke to the clang of metal on metal as the smithy
earned his living below. He rose to a seating position and
tested his arm; tentatively raising it above shoulder height.
He groaned and sucked the acrid air in through gritted teeth.
He took a sip from the tankard beside him; the cold water
soothed the harsh dry patches in the back of his throat. He
rolled back onto the straw bedding closed his eyes and wel-
comed sleep again. An unwelcome thought invaded his mind
once more. He cast it aside and refused to succumb to playful
temptation. The warmth of the furnace caressed his aching
bones and he lay in peaceful slumber. Still the thought per-
sisted. It pushed and pushed and would not stand idle; finally he could bear it no longer and he sat upright coughing; his
lungs fit to burst. He rubbed his eyes trying to clear the
smoke in front of him and shot out of the straw cot; even in
boots his feet felt the warm timber beneath him.He crossed
to the window and threw open the sash.

'Jack, Jack,' the smithy below was yelling up at the window,
'he's set the place alight come down, get out.'

Realisation crept over him as Jack took note of the foot steps
at the top of the stairs. He turned to see the massive frame of
Hobie Maxwell standing there in the room. Sword drawn,
held double handed, battle style.

'I hear you might be looking for me,' he stepped forward raising the huge sword.

Jack scooped up the tankard from beside the cot and hurled it towards his attacker. It smashed into his face, the remains of the water seeping into his matted hair. Jack watched the gargantuan frame recover, standing just as tall as before. A dark streak of blood formed across his blackened cheek.

'I'll spill your guts for that.' He raced across the room swinging the broad blade from side to side. Relentless anger powered each swipe, no thought or technique, just brute strength and perseverance at play. The sword cut into the timber frame around him and tore chunks of lime plaster from the walls.

Jack dodged and weaved around the sparsely furnished room; his precious Spanish rapier nowhere to be seen. He'd thrown what he could and took cover behind the central timber frame sprouting up from the room below. Each time Maxwell swung he over balanced so Jack lashed out with his good arm. The odd glancing blow wouldn't wear down Maxwell. The odds dictated that it would be over soon.

Thick black smoke now bellowed up the open staircase weaving its way around their feet but Maxwell still came forward. He slashed wildly, the open gash on his cheek pumped a steady stream of blood across his face; the red river coiling under his jaw, disappearing down the nape of his neck. Jack darted back and forth escaping the deadly arc of the swinging blade. His sword arm hanging limp by his side. The thud of sword on wood invaded their ears as Maxwell tried in vain to find some swinging space in the confines of the burning room. He came at him again and again thrusting the heavy blade forward. The 'swoosh' getting slower as Maxwell tired of swinging the sword. As Jack backed around the room he stumbled across the small chest containing his cloak and armour. The surroundings cursed him and he fell to the floor, his legs raised. Maxwell saw his chance, rushing forward; two hands on the hilt, the sword raised above his head the deadly blade pointing straight towards Jack.

'Go to your father'...

The blade soared forth but met only floor as Jack rolled to the side. He retrieved the dirk from his boot and clambered to his feet. He slammed the dagger into Maxwell's fleshy stomach. Again and again he stabbed. The sharp knife tore through the light tunic.

'Go to yours. If you have one,'

The tunic became thick with warm blood as he did his work. The crimson ale reached Jack's hand and he withdrew the knife. His frenzy abated. The crashing weight of his inevitable death flooded Maxwell's eyes with shock and he fell to his knees. His final gurgling cry was muffled by the sound of walls falling beneath them; the fire had quickly taken hold of the building. Jack fought through the black smoke as it rose upwards threatening to engulf the whole world. On reaching the window again he hauled himself outside and dropped onto the roof below. Smithy and his neighbours fought to contain the fire. Fetching water, removing hay. Jack struggled to his feet as Beth reached him. She recoiled at the wretched site of him. All blackened and bloodied. Smithy turned from the fire and walked towards Jack.

'I'm sorry about your home, smithy. I'll repay this debt,'

'It looks worse than it is. Look see, the hay is out now. I'll get in and put out the rest of it. You're still paying though.'

Jack smiled at that.

'Is it over?' Beth tentatively smiled at Jack.

The Warden approached from the crowd, flanked by two of his men. Swords sheathed but hands ready. Jack raised the bloody dirk; pointing the blade towards the Warden.

'The Pele house at East March belongs to the Hallden family. My family. It was put to flame along with my father Eric Hallden and the law did nothing. The three men who took it are dead. It now belongs to me along with their possessions their land and the cattle grazing at Ribbleshire valley. I will retrieve the cattle later myself.

'You propose too much,' The Warden stammered; trying to maintain some air of office.

'I propose to share the spoils with the smithy and the people helping him with the barn there. I'll divide the land into workable plots and they can pay me a fair rent if they want to take it on.' The folk turned their blackened faces away from the smouldering barn and came to stand beside Jack. The Warden seemed to understand. He would receive no quarter here. The balance had shifted; there was a new master.

'Very well, I will let it be known.' He turned sharply and walked off towards the tavern.

Jack winced as he tried again to move his sword arm. He managed, but the pain burned.

'Jack Hallden, you whine like a girl.' Beth playfully chastised him with a full smile.

'I think my arm is broken.' Jack cradled one arm in the other. 'And you would do well to treat me right. I'm a rich man now.' He teased through gritted teeth.

'Nonsense. Nothing but a flesh wound. And rich or poor you'll still find your way to my bed.'

'Shut up woman and fetch me an ale.'

It was good to be home.

Carol Fenlon

Carol lives in Skelmersdale where she hangs out with a crazy gang of writers and ponders on Freudian psychology. If writing is a sublimated activity as Freud claims does that mean all writers are sex starved? Her debut novel 'Consider The Lilies' won the Impress Prize 2007 and she has been publishing short dark fiction and poetry for more years than she cares to remember.

Half Known Things

It rained the day they buried Jamie Q. The whole estate turned out. After all, the kid had only been thirteen, caught in the crossfire. That was the official line, but on the estate people knew different. There was more to it than that.

People knew who had done it. Even Shirley knew. Wasn't her own Haydn knocking round with Flick Johnson, one of the fringe members of the Engineers?

But like Shirley, people only half knew. It was something you kept in a corner of your mind when you were chatting in the street or hoovering up: something you could banish altogether while Big Brother was on or while you were having a laugh at the pub quiz on a Thursday night. It was in those sleepless quiet hours when the kids were in bed that the worries came gnawing, about where you were and how safe you were. Shirley had many nights like that, wondering how she was going to make life work for Tonia, who was so light and pretty, so delicately beautiful that Shirley could scarcely believe that she and Pitt had actually produced her. Tonia's dreams were beautiful too, of riding horses, working in stables, even becoming a vet. This was what kept Shirley awake at night, trying to work out how to nurture Tonia as she prepared to blossom on the shit heap that was the estate.

Then there was Haydn, already well known to the police, running round with the Engineers, Flick Johnson knocking on the door. Look what had happened to Jamie Q. In her heart he was still her little boy, but she'd looked at him this morning in the churchyard, before he'd disappeared in the crowd, seen the beard trying to grow on his cheeks, seen the hardness already in his eyes and she'd known she was going to lose him.

Shirley let herself into her house, took off her coat and put the kettle on. It was only when she reached into her handbag

that she realized she was out of cigs. She could have done
with something stronger than coffee but there was nothing in
the house. She'd gone back to the Seven Stars after the funeral but it hadn't been the kind of send off where you sat round
eating sandwiches and getting pissed and shooting the shit
about what a good life the dead person had lived. Everyone
felt bad and didn't know what to say to the family because on
the one hand Jamie should have had all his life in front of
him but on the other he'd been a nasty piece of work even at
thirteen, already heavily involved with the Malt Way mob.

Shirley had felt herself in a funny position too, knowing how
Haydn was getting attached to the Engineers, she herself
working behind the bar in the Engine, the gang's home base.
She'd only eaten half an egg sandwich at the pub, and that
had stuck in her throat. She'd looked round for Haydn, hoping he'd come back with the crowd, but he'd gone off, probably to Pitt's even though he was supposed to stay with her
since his latest exclusion from school because Pitt's smack
habit and criminal record meant that he wasn't allowed to
have Haydn to stay. That was the official line, but Haydn
continually flouted it, abetted by Pitt and Shirley got tired of
trying to drag him back.

She went into his room looking for cigs. The mess in there
was in sharp contrast to the neatness of the rest of the house.
She rummaged through all the shit on top of the chest of
drawers, then opened the top drawer. It was as if it jumped
out and hit her in the chest. Her breath hitched in her throat,
then she laughed. It was a toy. She stretched out her hand. It
was real. She could tell by the serious cold feel of it. It was
black, dull, squat, like some horrid toad, something totally
alien in the homely mess of a young boy's bedroom.

'He's growing up. Going to the bad,' Shirley's mum kept saying, but it wasn't true. He was still just a child. Shirley pulled
her hand away. She wanted to pick it up, heft the weight to
test its reality, but she was desperately afraid of it. She closed

the drawer and backed out of the room, still staring through
the wood. She couldn't get the picture of it out of her mind.
Her breath was coming in gasps, her chest tightening and
squeezing. She crept down the stairs and into the kitchen, felt
in her handbag and took two puffs of her inhaler.

Haydn didn't come back all afternoon. Shirley waited for
Tonia to come home from school, smoking cig after cig and
watching out of the window for the flash of Haydn's purple
bike. She'd walked twice round the estate looking in his
favourite haunts to no avail. She'd thought she'd caught sight
of him and Flick Johnson riding away from the Engine but
there was no way she could run after them. Ahmad, the shop-
keeper said he'd come in around one o'clock with a couple of
the older Engineers.

'He's like the fucking invisible man.' Shirley tried to make a
joke but Haydn's badness and her own inability to control
him was in the way Ahmad looked at her and in the awkward
space across the counter between them. Like everyone else,
he half knew things. He had to make a living. She walked
home slowly, breath catching, hoping Ahmad hadn't been
able to see the picture in her mind. It was still so vivid, the
drawer opening, her hand reaching in.

Tonia bounced in at three thirty, still neat after a whole day
in her school uniform. She threw her school bag on the
kitchen table. 'Can I go to the library, Mum, I've finished   my
books?' She opened the fridge, poured herself a glass of Coke.

'You seen Haydn?' Shirley's chest tightened with the effort to
talk. Her whole body still seemed paralysed by the image of
the gun lying amongst Haydn's underpants. She reached for
the inhaler.

'No.' Tonia grimaced. 'Didn't he go with you?' She stood still
for a moment, even she knew about Jamie Q, but she wasn't
old enough to think much about death or to worry about

what had happened and whose fault it might be.

'Run off afterwards, didn't he?' Shirley lit another cig.
Tonia sighed. She hadn't much time for Haydn. 'He's a pig,
mum. Never mind.' She threw her arms round Shirley's neck,
then before Shirley could respond she was gone, skipping up
the stairs.

What if Tonia went in Haydn's room, opened the drawer?
Shirley's mouth went dry but she knew Tonia never went into
Haydn's room. When they'd both been small, he'd played
with her and she'd followed him everywhere but the last couple of years, since he'd started to change, get in with that bad
crowd, he'd ignored her at best and bullied her at worst, so
that the poor kid was half terrified of him now. She wouldn't
dare go in his room. But what if she did?

Tonia ran down the stairs just as Shirley heaved out of her
seat. Her arms were full of books. 'Please can I go to the
library, Mum?'

'I'm working.' Shirley stubbed out her cig. 'You're having tea
at your nan's, remember? She might take you after. It's open
late tonight. Be a good girl, go up and get washed and
changed.'

She waited until she could hear Tonia running the bathroom
taps, then she got her address book out of the kitchen drawer
and looked for the number. She picked up her mobile and
looked at the blank screen. She could see the gun lying in the
drawer. Tonia's books sat on the table. They all had pictures
of horses on the covers. Shirley lit another cig and called the
police.

<u>Danny King</u>

Danny King is the author of eight books, the
latest being Blue Collar. Before this he
worked for top literary tome, Club
International, where an earlier version of this
story first appeared. It is republished here
with big thanks to Rob Swift.

It Goes Where?

It makes me laugh all the controversy there is today surrounding the teaching of sex education to under-threes by
the PC brigade. See, it doesn't matter in the slightest what
age the government, your teachers or your parents decide
you're ready to hear about 'making babies', the chances are
your mates have got there first.

The fact is, it is you and your peers' responsibility to scare
the shit out of each other with wild stories about your geni-
tals and what are expected of them until school can get a
hold of you and set the record straight.

Peter Colson was the lad that pointed me in the wrong direction - him and Terry Allen. It was a lazy summer's afternoon
way back in 1979 and we were relaxing on top of a garage
roof after a leisurely mornings ant broiling. We were ten,
naive and, at the time, only casual smokers.

It all started with Terry: 'I hear you love Alison Pine,' he
sniggered, pointing the finger at me. This was fucking slan-
der. We were still at the age where all we wanted to do with
girls was push them off swings and kick them up the arse.
They were horrible and we hated them. Gangs of chubby little screechers who roamed the playgrounds looking for lads
to chase and kiss were the bane of our pre-hormonal existence. And they were getting worse. Recently they'd introduced pincer movements and ambush tactics into their game
so that hardly a day went by when we weren't pursued by a
flock of skirts intent on smothering us with sloppy kisses.

Alison Pine was a particularly feared specimen as she was
not only quick off the mark, she was also the class 'Flea-bag'.
And she was dangerously contagious, so that anything she
touched became instantly infected with fleas: her chair, her
bag, the door handle, anything. In fact whenever Alison Pine
shut a classroom door, the rest of the class couldn't get out

because no one else could touch the door handle without in turn becoming infected with fleas. This was how it worked and this situation was only ever resolved when the teacher stuck behind us would go fucking ballistic.

Of course, looking back on it there was nothing wrong with her really, but this was beside the point. As far as we were concerned her wayward brown hair hid a myriad of wildlife and when she did eventually wash it, it was with greasy chip wrappers and an old bike chain, so a block vote was taken to make her life a living hell to give her something to remember her early school days by.

Now, for some reason, even with all of this going on, our teachers would always ask Alison to hand out the books or the word sheets or the glitter or whatever else we were using that day, which protocol dictated could only be handled with just the thumb and forefinger and only at the very corners. Anyone who didn't follow these very strict hygiene guidelines obviously loved her and got tarnished with a dose of their own 'fleas' for a couple of days.

I'd been careless.

'No I don't, I hate her. I hate all girls,' I objected wildly, desperate to distance myself from the whiff of Flea-bag's popularity.

A certain amount of 'yes you do' no I don't' went on until Peter shattered our worlds forever by admitting he quite liked Jill Walker. Terry and me eyed Peter with horror. This was tantamount to confessing to being a Benny - tied to a tree or otherwise.

'Oh my God!' Terry exclaimed. 'You can't!' but he did. Peter told us the whole shameful truth. He'd been meeting up with Jill in secret, holding hands and even kissing her. On the lips!

This was too much to take. Peter of all people - what a poof! Of course I didn't fully understand what a poof was back then and this became apparent with my next declaration.

'I'll only ever go around with boys,' I said, and Terry agreed. But Peter wouldn't have it and he started us on a journey that would eventually lead to Terry's dismissal from the paint factory twenty years later for sexual harassment.

'You know when your willy gets stiff?' Peter said. I nodded having suffered from ice pops for many years myself. 'Well, that's girls who do that.'

'No they don't,' Terry countered. 'That's bicycle seats and buses.'

Peter shook his head. 'No, it's girls. Your willy gets stiff because girls make it go stiff.'

'How?' we asked, utterly perplexed as to how there could be a connection.

'They pray to make it happen and God does it,' Peter told us. This at least could've been true; I'd heard my mum through the bedroom wall on numerous Saturday nights pleading with the Almighty to give the old man the strength just once.

'But why?' Terry asked.

'Because you have to put it up their bum.'

Suddenly we realised that Peter had to be joking. I couldn't envisage any girl letting me stick my willy up her bum - and still can't in fact. 'I'm serious, that's how babies are made,' Peter insisted.

'Who told you that?' Terry demanded.

'My brother,' Peter replied and that confirmed it. Peter's brother knew everything. He was thirteen.

Terry asked how sticking one's willy up a girl's bum made a baby, though I immediately wished he hadn't. 'Stuff comes out of it,' Peter told us. 'Like tadpoles.'

'Tadpoles,' I gasped, suddenly petrified. At ten years old, the size difference between my knob and most tadpoles wasn't that significant.

'Flipping millions of them. They shoot out and go every-where. It's terrible.' Peter did me absolutely no favours here. For years afterwards I used to think that puddles of frog spawn were where perverts had just been having it off.

'And women like this?' I asked, shaking my head in disbelief.

'No of course they don't. But they do it if it means they get to marry you,' which made sense. Girls would do just about anything to marry boys. Terry said if this was the case he'd never get married, but Peter told him he couldn't avoid it that easily.

'When we go up to big school, we have to do sex education, and in the first lesson all the boys and girls in class have to line up naked in front of each other in the main hall. Then everyone has to go into a cubicle with a girl and do it with them. It's true, my brother told me.'

Resigned to our fate, Terry was the first to take whatever he could from a bad situation. 'Hope I get Sarah Donaldson,' he said.

'Hope I get Jill Walker,' Peter said.

'Bet I get Alison Pine,' I moaned.

We spent the rest of the afternoon roasting moss with our magnifying glasses, praying to God to protect us from girls and sacrificing dozens of small creatures to keep Him sweet.

Rather typically, this is the only prayer I've ever had answered.

Oh yes, and in case you're wondering, Alison 'Flea-bag' Pine grew up to be an absolute fucking stunner.

Stephen Cooper

Stephen has been hiding in Bulgaria for a while
now due to 'borrowing' a bike from an old mate
called Killer. He doesn't drink on Tuesdays as the
shipping forecast is most accurate on that particular evening. He enjoys 'silent but deadly' farts
beside women and has an abundance of ability in
the art of tree rubbing.He likes other stuff too.

<u>Justice</u>

Thursday again, I hate coming here.

The same imposing building, grey and horrible, glares back at me, almost sneering at my puny car in scale to its over-bearing gloom.

My best friend Keith is here. He wasn't always in here. I mean he wasn't always like this. I drive up to the entrance with a sense of both dread and hope. I dread seeing the other inmates; I have done ever since the first time I came here, but I have hope that someday I can get him out of here.

I remember that first visit. I made the mistake of not calling ahead, and ended up amidst the deranged and wailing, sick and demented souls in this hell hole. I walked, disorientated by the sheer size of the place, different floors, different wings, no signs to guide, and nobody I could ask in case they were also mad.

The sight will live with me, when I entered the ward for that first time, until I die. The first patient was on my right, eyes wide open at the shock of someone new, and he was red with exertion, masturbating furiously. I averted my eyes quickly to his right, there was another poor soul, dressed in a strait jacket, with a large padded helmet, repetitively head butting the wall, on and on, and on. The next one was wailing con-stantly, and at my appearance, his neighbour ran towards me, covered in human excrement, his hands waving above his head. I threw up, the putrid stench overpowering my senses, and before I even finished heaving, several others had joined him on their hands and knees on the floor, examining the remnants of my lunch.

I turned, ran outside, and threw up again. I didn't go back in that day, just drove home in a deeply shocked state, thinking I would never see my mate again.

It took me several phone calls and five days before I summoned up the courage to venture over here again. The head nurse, Helen, a motherly type, as you would imagine, deserves and receives my unstinting admiration for the life she leads for the benefit and loving care of others. How anyone can endure this day after day is something I cannot really understand.

Most days we sit outside on the veranda, it has a roof in case it rains and a path that we can use together. Keith is in a wheelchair; I can take him down to our special summer seat, and chat for as long as we want. Keith doesn't really say much, he has withdrawn from himself, apparently a common symptom after suffering a breakdown.

He's been here now for three and a half years after his wife's suicide - and approx three years, and eight months after his daughter's rapist walked off scot free from the courtroom. He was supposed to pick his daughter, Amy up on the night in question from a disco, but ended up worse for wear at his Christmas work do, and fell asleep on the sofa.

She was easy prey for the monster that followed her the three miles home and raped her at knifepoint in the woods beside our football pitches. The clever bastard had prepared his chloroform soaked handkerchief, and used it quickly and efficiently. Amy came to, just as he was withdrawing and of course started to scream. A blow to knock her unconscious took care of that and in a blind panic, the assailant stabbed her viciously five times.

He then proceeded to calm down and brutalize her in the most sickening manner. Amy was left with a deep incision to each breast; her genitalia ruptured by his knife and twisted to ensure she would be forever childless.

He then made good his escape.

Amy was found unconscious a number of hours later by an inquisitive springer spaniel just after six am, the loss of blood had rendered her almost certainly dead. Her good fortune that day was that the dog's owner was a paramedic coming off shift, and his prompt mobile phone call and subsequent actions almost certainly saved her life.

Even so, it was eight months before fourteen year old Amy went back to school.

It was his smell and his eyes that gave him away, even though he wore a hat and scarf to hide his identity. Amy recognized him a couple of weeks after returning to school. It was chemistry class, he leaned over her to correct her Bunsen burner and she freaked out. That smell, and the eyes up close, everything came at a rush, the realization the monster was here, the shock made her fall off her stool.

Of course, nobody believed her; silly teenage girls never are taken seriously. Hysterical and distraught, Amy refused to go back to school and disappeared for the last two months of the last year she had left. No exams, no future. Her best friend took her in, and unknown to Keith at first, proceeded to encourage a legal case against 'Mr. Chemistry'.

Keith never forgave himself, and his late wife Caroline, never did either. Days and weeks in the aftermath, alcohol and drugs added to the growing distance between them and pushed them further apart.

Only two months after the stress, strain and extreme let down of the court case, Caroline emptied a concoction of pills into her tiny frame and washed it down with a bottle of whiskey, and a few mouthfuls of bleach for good measure, to leave this world behind.

Keith found her the next morning, coming in from nightshift, and never really got over it. Amy was taken into care, after social services added to his woes and officially judged him to be an 'unfit father', and Keith unsurprisingly, went further downhill.

After the funeral, I took Keith in with me in my flat, I was on my own, as my wife had the sense to leave me years ago, and I didn't mind the company if I am honest. Around three months later, after almost drinking himself into a stupor, Keith had his breakdown.

After showering as usual, he cut off most of his hair in the bathroom mirror, shaved off all bodily hair, including even his eyebrows, and still dripping wet, proceeded to walk down the main street of the village with head strangely to one side and a vacant stare on his face.

The Post Office was as far as he got, and the poor sod was lifted by my colleagues and brought into the sorting room, where I had started my shift. We got him sorted with spare clothes and I took him to hospital in my post van.

Tony, his dad has never really recovered either. A self made man, he's established an export business from scrap metal. Cars of all types are regularly stripped and crushed in his scrap yard and sent to China. Many a time Tony told me he could do just the very same to himself, become a square block and get sent far away to the far east, away from the shattered fragments of his bereft existence.

Nurse Helen encourages me to visit as often as possible. I could come more often, but, the truth is, it breaks my heart.

Keith and I grew up together, played for the same football team, drank together, we were best men at our weddings for each other and I can't think of anyone I was ever closer to.

To see him in this state is hard to take. Most days, I find it difficult to hold it together, and have resorted to smoking cigarettes to stop my lip trembling and breaking down. We sit on our special summer seat, Keith sits beside me in his wheelchair pulled up close with his tartan rug, his favourite cap on, and I try to coax memories out of him. I will probe with anything, ex girlfriends, football, his late mum, old jokes, teachers; I am desperate.

Some days I get a reaction, a brief flicker in those lifeless eyes, but most days they stay dead, like muddy stagnant water.

The worst is when Nurse Helen comes walking down the path, Keith can see her, and knows our time is up, and he puts his right arm around me, and leans in close and moans softly. He can still speak, but not very coherently, 'stay', and 'don't go' are like sentences from him now. I am not ashamed to tell you I cant think of anything else so painful I will have to endure in my life, than to hear those words pierce and twist my heart like they do.

And they do, every single week.

I come every Thursday, it's a sort of routine now, and I spend the afternoon here.

After its time for me to leave, I say my goodbyes and kiss my mate's forehead, and he sobs, like a wee boy as Helen wheels him away up the path into oblivion for another week.

I silently cry the whole way to my car, and sit for anything up to thirty minutes before I can drive, or rather, before I can see through my blurred eyes well enough to drive back home.

The emotions I go through driving home are remarkably potent, even now after nearly four years. The frustration of watching my best friend like this, and not being able to do anything is indescribable. I get angry, I find myself getting cramps in my hands due to unwittingly gripping my steering wheel so tight, I feel sorrow, deep sorrow, and finally shame.

I feel shame because sometimes I have to deal with battling thoughts of not wanting to go back, because I don't want the pain anymore. When I think like that, I hate myself for even contemplating it.

I dump my car, and I head to my local, the Dragon, to meet with Tony, Keith's dad. Every week I sit and reminisce with him. I think it helps us both, but sometimes it's tough. Thursday night is quiz night. I join in. I don't contribute very much; my knowledge is limited to probably just the local geography due to my job as postman, sport, and maybe the odd history question.

As for my job, I am in the sorting office around five am, on the street around seven, and finished around one in the afternoon. My best friend in work is my thermos flask, full of piping hot tea, and safely ensconced in my van. The simple things in life are the most valuable I muse, especially now in the run up to Christmas, when it's freezing cold.

Tonight, though, it's different. I need to talk to Tony; I have a favour to ask from him, I need an old battered car for a couple of days. Tony doesn't ask me why I want it, I have become like a second son since his own son's demise, I suppose some people would say a surrogate. We arrange the logistics; I will pick it up next week, before it gets crushed into three cubic feet of metal, ready for the long boat to China next Friday.

I have a bit of work to do next week. I happened to come across something quite shocking around two months ago in the sorting office in the neighbouring district, where I was covering for a colleague on a course.

I was getting my letters and parcels ready when I was visibly shocked to find a name on a letter I hadn't seen in quite a while. In fact, it was three years and a bit since I registered that name. The realization that Amy's attacker was living in my delivery run shook me up totally.

The first few times I had to actually physically deliver the various letters into his letter box, after walking up his path, I could feel my heart pumping in my ears. Amy's former chemistry teacher lives in a small flat and had moved on to another area, probably complete with decent references from the previous school. Innocent until proven guilty they probably said, and all that usual nonsense.

A month or so into the run he had spoken to me coming out of his drive, and now, I am on speaking terms with him on a regular basis. He will have to sign for a parcel next week. I know his routine very well. He leaves the house at around half seven every morning and I have arranged to bring it next Thursday.

He doesn't know yet he isn't really getting a parcel, or at least, not the sort of parcel he thinks normal postmen deliver.Then again, I am not a normal postman, not now I know where he lives.

*****

I arrive in Tony's battered old Astra, a real heap of shit, probably gone round the clock two or three times and park in the old restaurant car park two blocks away. I haul my post bag containing the 'parcel' along to my recipient. I am wearing my uniform as usual, I won't raise any eyebrows, and I have worn gloves and clothes I won't need after this very special delivery.

I ring his doorbell, its seventeen minutes past, just a bit early on purpose. He arrives at the door, humming some dopey tune, thinking about the day ahead in his dressing gown and dripping from the shower. I drop my post bag, and with a sudden ferocious surging head butt to his nose,down he goes and in I go.

In my post bag I have a large area of plastic tarpaulin, some rope, some smelling salts, some masking tape, a sock, and a very large, serrated edged, knife.

I've been waiting a long time for this, and I am going to do this bastard proper.

He comes to his senses in the kitchenette. He is puzzled to find he is sitting on a chair, bound, gagged, naked and surrounded by plastic on the floor. I spend some time with him telling him exactly who I am. I spend a further few minutes applying a tourniquet to his femoral artery. It's difficult as he tries to kick and fight and I get fed up and plant him a rabbit punch to his temple.

His eyes, wide with terror, signal that he's awake via my smelling salts. He probably wishes he hadn't came around again. I show him my knife. I explain what I am going to do and his moans reach a high whimper and his bowels join in with the symphony.

Urine and excrement drip from the plastic chair, reminding me of the stench from my first visit where my best mate is stuck because of this excuse of a human being, I can't help but feel the utmost loathing for this object.

And it is an object now; it is no longer a life form worthy of the air that we breathe.

I kick back the chair. He passes out when his head hits the scullery floor. Then I bend over his limp unconscious body, and I cut neatly into his scrotum, and remove his testicles. I place them on his chest; they are like little white Brussels sprouts dipped in ketchup, I wouldn't like to try them though.

Then I have an idea. I tighten the tourniquet and cut his flaccid penis like a butcher cuts a piece of meat, quickly and without fuss. I know now what I will do next. I place my knife in through the masking tape over his stupid gob, and remove the sock from his mouth.

I pop in his limp little cock, the same little cock which is responsible for everything, and mask his mouth up again with the tape, nice and neat.

Then I release the tourniquet and the blood begins to ooze out of his gaping penal hole. The smelling salts bring him around to hell. I am sure even he could never imagine an ending like this. In between consciousness he is delirious and I am reveling in my roles as the judge, the jury and the executioner today.

I tell him what is in his mouth, he passes out. I revive him time and time again, goading him with my knife, like he probably did to little Amy, until finally, his body surrenders.

I sever his carotid artery, and the blood sprays out like a fountain, and I watch his last throes, before wrapping up the body in the polythene and clean up.

For a little man, he's surprisingly heavy. I carry him to the waiting Astra, bemused by the fact that such an old banger is carrying its equivalent in quality of human life.

I return the car to Tony's scrap yard, lock it up and take the keys and my contaminated clothing home. It takes me twenty three minutes to get there. I burn my clothes and scrub myself clean in the shower with a solution of disinfectant and water.

No one will miss the guy for a week, there won't be any letters being delivered for that long at least, I can personally guarantee that.

***

Today is Thursday, and off I go after work to see Keith. He is his normal self, we chat, and he listens with his eyes dull, but he feels secure beside me, his best mate still. In the aftermath of the court case, and when we were living together and sharing the pain, I promised him that if I ever found Amy's attacker, I would tell Keith. I imagined what he wanted to do with him. Today, I wonder if he would have done what I just have. I eventually come into reality and out of my thoughts when I see Nurse Helen is coming up the path.

I lean over to him.

Keith like every other week has his arm around me, the right one, as usual, and before he can moan or speak, I place both of mine around him and I whisper into his ear, 'Justice.'

For the first time in almost four years, he turns and looks me squarely in my eyes, and I see his twinkle and I feel him chuckle. I hug him tight, tears silently seeping down our cheeks.

Nurse Helen tells me in parting I have seemed to have made a difference today.

As its Thursday I go to meet Tony, I will stick to my plan, follow the discipline, that's how you beat the police and the rest of them. When I sit down in the Dragon, I want to throw my arms around Tony, and tell him what I have done. I push my feelings away, go for a piss and throw some cold water on my face to get a grip. When I come back, a pint of Guinness is in front of me. He tells me, with a smile that almost covers the pain in his eyes, how many times he remembers me and Keith drinking Guinness together,

'I wish I had a pound for every one you two used to have'.

I almost start to cry, I love this man, and I can see through the forced smile and the sorrow inside his empty soul. Instead, I light a cigarette, and I buy him a drink and control my trembling lip.

*****

Driving home from the pub, the radio is playing annoying Christmas songs. Every year they play this crap, do they have any heart? I turn it off and we travel in comfortable silence. I can't help it, but I need some confirmation that I covered myself properly.

'By the way, Tony,' I glance sideways, 'forgot to ask, did you get the Astra back alright in the yard?'

He glances out the window 'Aye, its now three cubic feet of scrap metal, and on the slow boat to China,' he says with a laugh.

I should shut up and leave it, but I just can't help myself.

'Do you get much for a cubic three feet of squashed car'?

'A bit better now, but the transport is getting expensive son.' He replies.

'I hope you got a good price for the Astra.'

Puzzled, he turns to look at me. 'Why's that, son? It was a heap of crap.'

I keep my eyes glued to the road.

'It's just that they got a couple of extra feet in the boot with that one.'

The passing neon lights show my best mate's father with a

heavy sigh opening his eyes, the world lifted off his shoulders. His cheeks are glistening with the tears of relief, captive for four years, and he is smiling, but this time it's a proper heartfelt smile.

'Justice.' I whisper.

Tony leans across and puts his right arm around my shoulder.

Like father - like son.

Ken McCoy

Ken is actually a builder who took the winter off due to a downturn in the building industry. That's the downturn in '92 by the way!
He missed the recent building boom due to being busy writing his fourteen (that's 14!) books and is being told that now's not a great time to be going back into the industry. Bugger eh! Ah well, back to the scribbling Ken.

Mikhail

It was almost midnight and they were here again, outside his
front door. He knew they'd come. He hoped they'd come. But
that didn't mean he wasn't scared. They were yelling and
whooping like American golf fans only these boys weren't
American, nor were they fans of anything except alcohol,
skunk, sex and gratuitous violence against anyone weaker
than themselves. They hunted in a pack because individually
they didn't amount to much, and they called themselves the
Skag Crew. Half of them had ASBOS against them and several others wore tags which they managed to circumvent, much
to the frustration of the police.

The Elmhurst housing estate was their territory and they
infested it like foul and feral dogs. They peddled drugs;
mugged anyone they thought might be worth mugging, or
simply just for fun, and they vandalised any dwelling not
occupied by one of their crew or any car not owned by them.
In short they were a law unto themselves because the police
considered the Skag Crew to be relatively minor offenders,
albeit prolific. To bring them to book would take manpower
the police didn't have, plus they were unlikely to get custodial
sentences due to prison overcrowding.

The respectable residents did their best to turn a blind eye,
as experience told them that getting involved or reporting
them to the police would only make them targets. On the
occasions when members of the Skag Crew had found themselves in court, witnesses had a tendency not to turn up.
Intimidation was rife on the Elmhurst.

Arthur had stood up to them once when they'd all lined up
outside his front window and showed their naked backsides
to his wife, Eileen, who had inadvertently looked out to see
what the noise was. He had gone out and faced them, told
them to get back under the stones they'd crawled out from
under. He'd made the mistake of taking an old golf club with

him, just in case they turned nasty. As a young man he'd
served, with some distinction, in Korea so he wasn't scared of
a bunch of yobbos.

Their leader, the loudest and biggest, called himself the Skag.
He had walked up to him and spat in his face. Arthur had
brandished the golf club but Skag had brushed it aside and
head-butted him. He had lost consciousness and fell to the
ground with blood pouring from his broken nose. Eileen had
gone out to help. As she knelt beside him they'd all danced
around her, then some of them urinated on her as she tried
to bring him round. Their laughter was obscene and it was
the worst moment of her life.

The police took the youths in for questioning but they all said
Arthur had started it by attacking them with a golf club.
They'd denied the urinating bit with it being Eileen's word
against theirs. There had been evidence on her clothes but
she'd declined the offer to have them forensically examined.
She simply wanted the matter to end. Despite this, Arthur
was taken in for questioning regarding his alleged attack with
the golf club. He was held overnight before being let off with
a severe warning to let the police do the job next time.

 Arthur had no doubt some of the neighbours would have
witnessed it but they were all too scared to get involved. The
estate had been built in the sixties when the future was concrete and architects viewed the world from halfway up their
arses. They had assumed that everyone would want to live on
top of each other in colourless concrete gulags with walkways
and balconies and underground passages and bare, concrete
walls begging to be defaced with illiterate and obscene grafitti.

Arthur and his wife had been moved out of their terraced
house due to a Compulsory Purchase Order and had been
imprisoned here on the Elmhurst Estate. His old address had
been 23 Elmhurst Avenue but now it was 48b Elmhurst

Mansions. His old street had been cobbled and they had known all the neighbours, some of whom had lived there since he was a boy, as had he. He vividly remembered the street party in May 1945, to celebrate VE Day. It was the day he'd got his call-up papers to go and join the army. He spent most of his national service helping to deal with displaced persons in Poland. In 1947 he signed up for a further six years, ending up in Korea. On the very day he came home, with his Distinguished Service Medal, there was another street party, partly for him, partly to celebrate the Coronation of Queen Elizabeth II. But all these memories were now blighted with what the powers-that-be had seen fit to replace Elmhurst Avenue and the surrounding streets.

Many of the dwellings on the stark estate were boarded up due to vandalism. The walls were covered in obscene grafitti and stank of urine. He lived on the ground floor which, at first, he'd thought the best place to live out his and Eileen's old age. No stairs to climb, no broken down lifts to worry about and it had looked okay. It had a neat kitchen and storage heaters and it wasn't far from the shops. It was now though. All the useful shops had closed down, priced out by the supermarkets or forced out by vandalism. He couldn't afford a car so all the shopping was done by bus. He always went with Eileen, she couldn't have carried a week's shopping on her own. Quite often, on the way back they'd have to run the gauntlet of howling, spitting youths. Eileen had often been in tears when they got in and he felt he'd let her down for not being able to afford a decent home for her to spend her twilight years.

Sometimes the Skag would sell drugs right outside his window, in the full knowledge that Arthur could see what was going on. On more than one occasion he'd found excrement pushed through his letter box. The Skag Crew would congregate there and make his life a misery with their noise until the early hours. He'd called the police but the police always arrived with sirens howling, giving them plenty of warning to clear off. A few, stealthy, silent cars would have been the obvious way to catch them but it was as if the police didn't want a confrontation. Sometimes it seemed as if the police didn't believe him when he told them what had been happening.

'If you want to catch them at it you'll have to drive up quietly,' he'd told them. But the officers would look at each other as if to say, 'Who the hell does he think he is, telling us our job?'

Somehow they'd found out that it was Eileen's 80th birthday. The youths had parents, and parents knew people who knew Eileen, and so Skag and his crew found out it was her birthday. He and Eileen had celebrated it on their own because she was never one for a fuss. They had a son but he was in Australia. He'd sent her a beautifully framed photograph of himself, his wife and their two boys, who were themselves grown up. Eileen had treasured it and gave it pride of place on top of the television.
That night, just before midnight, they had gone to bed. Eileen was curled up in his arms and they'd talked about the old days, when they were childhood sweethearts, back in the thirties. There had been no trouble from the Skag Crew for quite a few nights and Arthur said maybe they were growing out of it. Eileen was saying she hoped so when they heard a knock on the door. She looked at the illuminated dial on the clock. 11.55.

'Oh, God, Arthur. I do hope it's not them.'

But the knock had seemed polite. More of a neighbourly knock. Arthur went to the door but didn't open it. He just shouted, 'Who's there?', but there was no reply. Then he noticed a parcel had been pushed through the letter box. It was addressed to his wife in very neat handwriting. Such neat writing must have been done by someone with an educated mind. It wasn't the illiterate scrawl of a mindless yob.

He took it through to Eileen saying she must have a mystery admirer. She smiled at his joke.

'What? At this time of night? I'm a bit past having admirers now. '

'I think it might be from Molly Hargreaves,' Arthur said. 'Her and Billy will have been passing on the way back from the Crown and Anchor.'

She took off the brown paper wrapping, inside which was a slim, white, cardboard box, the type an expensive birthday card might come in. She took the lid off, then shrieked in horror as the cockroaches poured out running all over the bed, down her nightie, all across the floor, dozens of them. She screamed and wept in terror and despair then she jumped out of the bed, beating the roaches off her nightie. Arthur tried to help but as he did she collapsed to the floor with a massive stroke that killed her instantly. Her bereft husband knelt beside her and hugged her to him, but her body was limp. Outside the window he could hear loud guf-faws of laughter fading into the night as Skag and his crew went on their way. Their night's entertainment off to a good start. Arthur wept as he tried to brush the roaches off Eileen's hair and her nightdress. He knew he should call an ambulance but he didn't want to leave her to the mercy of the bugs. He tried to give her the kiss of life. He thumped on her chest to get her heart started then he picked her up and car-ried her through to the hall where the phone was. No way would he leave her on her own. But Eileen was dead, he knew that. She'd died of fright at the hands of Skag and his crew. Just to amuse them.

*****

Three months had passed and nothing had been done to the youths who had killed his wife; the animals who had scared her to death on her birthday. The police were sympathetic

but there was nothing they could do. It was an idiotic prank
perpetrated by idiotic youths who all denied it. They'd left no
prints on the parcel or the box inside, and even if they had it
was doubtful if the courts would send any of them down.
Eileen had died of a stroke, simple as that. She hadn't been
the victim of a physical assault, just a mindless prank.

Today was Arthur's birthday and he wondered if they had a
prank to play on him. His son had come over from Australia
for the funeral and had tried to persuade Arthur to go back
with him, but to him this was tantamount to deserting Eileen
and giving in to the people who had killed her. She wouldn't
want to give them the satisfaction. He'd bought himself a
nice birthday present from an old army pal of his down at the
British Legion who had been reluctant to let it go.

'I've grown very fond of it over the years, Arthur. I always felt
safe with him in the house.'

'Him? It's a he is it? I thought it was a she.'

'No, Arthur, it's definitely a he. His name's Mikhail. He's
Russian and he's a bugger when he gets going.'

'I've heard they all are.'

'Only in the right hands, Arthur. He needs treating properly.
By the way, if he gets you into trouble I know nothing about
him. You didn't get him from me.'

'Why, is he illegal?'

'He's very illegal, Arthur.'

Arthur smiled when he got Mikhail home and he stroked him
with immense satisfaction and promised he'd take him out
for some exercise, probably later that night when it was dark.

Arthur had been very free with his accusations about who
was responsible for his wife's death. Skag and his crew were
not pleased. Everyone on the estate seemed to know the
truth but no one said it to their faces. No one dared, but they
knew. Skag and his crew also knew that it was Arthur's birthday and Arthur suspected that they knew.

Just before midnight, around the same time that Eileen had
died, a brick came though his front room window. Arthur
had been lying in bed, dozing. The noise brought him fully
alert. He got of bed, put on his coat and, with Mikhail by his
side, he went to the front door and cautiously looked out.
Skag and his crew were there in force, yelling and whooping,
drinking beer out of cans and spitting in his direction. Some
looking around at neighbouring windows and snarling at
anyone who dared to look out. Watching faces disappeared.
Whatever happened here would do so without witnesses.

Skag spoke, belligerently. 'Now then you old twat. What's all
this crap about us killin' yer wife?'

'It's true,' said Arthur, evenly. There was no fear in his voice,
which angered Skag. He was used to people being scared of
him.

'Oh, yeah. Where's yer witnesses?'

Arthur made no reply.

'This is the Elmhurst Estate,' sneered Skag. 'No one witnesses
anything on the Elmhurst, not if they've got any sense.'

He took a couple of steps towards Arthur, the group moved
with him. Skag took out a flick knife and snapped it open. It
glinted in the lamplight as he jabbed it within a few inches of
Arthur's face. Arthur didn't flinch, nor did he move back
inside as Skag might have expected. He brought Mikhail out
in front of him. Skag backed away, as did the crew. Arthur

pulled Mikhail's trigger and fired off a dozen accurate rounds into the youths to Skag's right. They all fell to the ground, dead. Skag flung his hands in the air in horror as did the five surviving youths. Arthur pointed the weapon, invented by Mikhail Kalashnikov in 1947, at Skag and took a step towards him. He spoke in the same unafraid, even voice.

'The most dangerous man you'll ever come across is a man with nothing to lose, lad, and I'm just that man. You've made the mistake of taking everything from me, so now I'm going to return the favour.'

The six surviving youths were paralysed with fear. Even in the lamplight they could see death in Arthur's eyes. Their death. Six of their gang were already dead. Arthur fired a prolonged burst at the youths to Skag's left, bringing four of them down. Ten dead now. Skag and the other survivor dropped to their knees weeping in abject terror, but the only thought in Arthur's mind was of how his wife of fifty three years had died because of their cruelty.

He fired another burst which almost cut Skag's companion in two. Leaving Skag on his own. He knelt with his head in his hands, sobbing with fear, wetting himself. Arthur took a cloth from his pocket and calmly wiped all his fingerprints from the gun. He looked around and noticed, with some satisfaction that no faces were at any of the windows. No one wanted any of the bullets heading their way and who could blame them? To them it meant the Skag Crew had graduated to guns. Time to keep your heads down, neighbours. Don't get involved with this. Skag's terrified eyes followed Arthur, who was wandering among the carnage he had created; checking that they were all dead. They were. He slammed in a fresh magazine then he flung Mikhail on the ground in front of Skag.

'There you are, lad. If you're man enough, take a pop at me!'

Skag looked at the AK47 on the ground in front of him. It's curved magazine pointing at him. He wondered what the catch was. His mind was in a turmoil and he couldn't think straight. So he wasn't thinking when he picked up the gun and emptied the whole magazine into Arthur who dropped to his death among the Crew. Skag was struggling to his feet, semi-paralysed with shock when the police arrived, sirens screaming. The sight that met them was a known thug and drug dealer standing there with an AK47 in his hands, in the midst of a bloodbath. Eleven youths and one old man, all shot dead with bullets from the weapon he was holding. They shouted at him to drop the gun, which he did.

More police cars arrived. He would tell them an unbelievable story of how a frail, eighty year old man with no criminal record had done all this, not him. However he struggled to explain how the old man had managed to empty a full magazine into his own body without leaving any of his fingerprints on the gun. The only prints on the gun were Skag's. Twelve people were dead. Someone had to carry the can - the can being twelve life sentences with no hope of parole - ever, which is a long time in jail when you're only nineteen. A witness would have been handy for Skag. But this was the Elmhurst Estate where no one witnesses anything.

Not if they've got any sense.

<u>Roz Goddard</u>

Roz is a former poet laureate of
Birmingham and has the distinction of doing a
reading in a thunderstorm whilst being heckled by
a drunk with his top off. Her latest collection,
'How to Dismantle a Hotel Room', contains a
poem which imagines Reggie Kray getting
annoyed as he plays scrabble in Heaven. Available
from the website www.rozgoddard.com

The Lexus gives off an Aura

I am expecting a visit from the local councillor. She has rung
ahead like the gas man and said I can expect her in twenty
minutes. She is a capable woman, a cabinet member with
responsibility for education - she has not yet reached the
stage where her ambition takes precedence over the concerns
of her constituents. She responds promptly to e-mails
(abbreviates nothing) and walks the delicate line between
professionalism and human warmth. According to the local
paper she has 'battled' breast cancer and is 'determined to
continue to provide a listening ear' to the people who have
voted for her. The speed bumps in our road are down to her.
I love it when a pimply youth, hunched over the wheel of
some sporty monstrosity, is forced to slam on the brakes -
sending his baseball cap flying. I explained to Councillor
Liddy that there is now a new problem - namely local youths
caterwauling and lighting fires in the park. My blood pres-
sure is being adversely affected; I can show her the charts,
the spikes - 175/120, 161/98. When they clink past with their
carrier bags of alcohol, I can feel my arteries tightening. The
park is not the carefree place it once was. It is where youths
with too much time on their hands sit under shady trees and
drink lager, it is where scowling young men take their bull
terriers to terrorise ordinary folk and it is where my neighbours have illicit sex.

I spotted Helen and Brian while I was on a fungi hunt - in a
part of the park that borders a nature reserve, off the normal
run, where you might fancy you were back in the territory of
your childhood. You cannot hear the roaring cars, or see
tower blocks choking the sky. You can just about make out
the fall of the Brook over the old stones. I was aware of a
rustling of leaves and girlish giggling near by. I moved into a
position up on a small rise where I could see them quite
clearly and there was Brian - one hand against the ancient
bark and the other disappeared up Helen's skirt. She moved
oddly to one side and then I realised it was to give him

greater access. I gripped my bag of Ceps and tumbled off through the leaves and thought I heard stifled laughter as I retreated.

Helen is married to Jim, she teaches chess in the local primary schools and he is in publishing. 'What kind of publishing?' I asked her once. 'English as a second language,' she said. He's quite high up, has to go off to Spain and Dubai on missions. I googled him once, there he was, 'James Eliot' Commissioning Editor, Anderson-Sinclair. He looked pleased with himself and more like an alpha male on the screen than he does in real life, his gaze was steady and confident - authoritative, clearly in work mode. I used to watch him putting his brief case in the boot of his car, he struck me then as needing to put weight on; what is it with workaholics - haven't they got time to eat? No time to eat, no time to talk. There was no point trying to engage him in conversation on a Sunday morning - he took an age to wash his black Lexus, lavishing it with a long, lazy motion of the arm, dancing around it, sweeping back and forth.

'You can come and do mine if you like,' I'd shout over, he'd look at me and his mouth would go up just on the one side - more a twitch than a smile. The one time I did get a peep out of him, was when I was getting a petition up to send to the councillor, 'It's a nightmare,' he said, 'nightmare,' and signed my petition with a flourish. I thought that a rather bland response for someone who dealt in words for a living. Helen signed too. She looked unhappy as she leant on my clipboard to sign and her skin was the colour of porridge - I could hear the kids shrieking in the garden, perhaps they were getting on her nerves. I have never been into their house, but I could see the warm glow coming from the sitting room when I walked past in the evening - and the books - they must have bought them by the yard.

With Brian, Helen was re-born, I could see the gloss on her hair from across the street. Regular as clockwork he'd saunter down the street when the Lexus wasn't there, eager, taking a moment to look at the sky, like he was savouring the world. She'd open the front door and their dark shapes would linger for a moment in their customary greeting, then disappear from the frosted glass.

A couple of Christmases ago I went out shopping for underwear and ingredients to make a cake. I lingered around the knickers in Debenhams and was dumbfounded at the range of lacy confections. They didn't do them in my size but I picked out two sets anyway (I've always been an optimist) one black and one red - and threw in some beautiful stockings with a dark seam running up the back. Trundling home with my bursting bags I felt full of joy, yes that's not too strong a word for it - it was like being on the eve of something. My plan was to bake the cake, shower, change and go over to Brian's bearing gifts. Since his wife had shipped out, he'd let things slip, his hedge was full of crisp packets and the net curtain in his bathroom was getting blacker. I didn't want to rescue him, don't think that. I knew what it was to walk between cold rooms, to feel time on my back, maybe we could be a comfort to one another.

I put on some Jamie Cullum, lit candles and sang in the jasmine smelling shower, it was like being very young again when there is a great glowing bulk of pleasure just ahead of you and you are about to walk right into it and you know it will be wonderful. At last. I tottered round to his place in a pair of patent shoes I'd pulled from the cupboard, there were carol singers going up and down the street, the evening was unseasonably warm and they were singing between calls, giving the street free songs, it seemed like a wonderful omen. His car was on the drive, I knew he was in. I rang the bell and when he opened the door a bachelor coldness came from the hall behind him. 'I don't seem to be able to get my lawn mower moving - I wondered if you could look at it for me?' That's the first thing I said before offering him the cake. 'Come in, come in,' he said and before I knew it I was sitting

in his coolish lounge drinking parsnip wine and he was
telling me about his plans to emigrate. He'd got family in
Australia who needed help running a sheep farm in
Queensland. 'It's now or never Liz,' he said.

'Take me to bed,' I said.

There were oblong spaces on the walls where he'd started
taking down his pictures, some of them were leaning against
sofas and chairs. He reached for one, it was a sentimental
photograph of a dog sitting patiently on the worn step of a
pub looking into the camera with moony eyes, it said, 'His
Master's Vice' underneath. 'Please have this.' He said. It was
obviously inappropriate, he was using a tactic that mothers
of toddlers use when they want to distract them or shut them
up, 'Or this.' He thrust a Patrick Caulfied print of lots of different coloured pots battling for space, at me. 'What varied
taste you have.' I said. He started stammering then, as if
words were fighting in his throat and he didn't know which
ones to pull free. I think he said he was flattered, but he
turned off the Ella Fitzgerald we'd been listening to and sat
there with his legs crossed. 'Enjoy the cake,' I said, before
leaving.

Our houses are in a decent Crescent, with a good amount of
space between them, people haven't gone mad with throwing
up extensions - we are a road of stayers, some of us have
been here for years. Can you imagine knowing nothing about
your neighbours? It wouldn't be right - you need to know a
bit about their habits and foibles - otherwise you're unteth-
ered, floating, clueless. The Blakes live at number twenty
four, he took redundancy years ago and hasn't worked since -
he collects wood for his open fire and leaves great branches
on the drive, they have two Dalmatians - Prince and Duke -
who they dote on, though he does all the dog walking, she's
overweight and has people come to the house for hopi ear
candle therapy. The Pearces live at twenty seven, again he
doesn't work, he used to be on the production line at Rover

and hasn't worked since the redundancies. She's a nurse, they have adopted a little lad called Stephan who screams blue murder every early evening around six, poor thing, still getting used to a strange house I would imagine. I'm monitoring that situation and won't hesitate to contact the authorities if I have to. Brian decided that The Crescent had certain attractions - he didn't emigrate to Australia after all.

One day Jim's Lexus stayed on the drive, it was there the next day and the next. Cars speak too, they ooze communication. The impressive looking machine waited that day, stoically, rain bouncing off its roof, redundant on the tarmac while the little universe of Helen and Jim's family fell apart. The children went to school - a woman who looked like Helen with the same pompous bearing, came to pick them up - while Helen and Jim stayed in the house, presumably, to talk about what they were going to do. The letter would have arrived with the other brown envelopes and junk. I decided to write and tell Jim what I'd seen because he'd be dead soon - furred arteries, air travel, bad diet and stress - and it angered me that serene, chess playing Helen would have got away with murder. I know what you're thinking - frustrated, spurned spinster wants to stop other people having what she can't. You're right, it's true. You read a lot of rubbish about getting beyond your negativity, moving on, live and let live. Where's the reckoning? If it's in the next world for Helen, I won't bloody well see it will I? But I can see her wan face, the way her hair hangs limp. I can see that the early evening lights don't go on in her front room these days, the books are in shadows and the Lexus is elsewhere in the city, going round in circles avoiding home for long hours. That's a kind of justice.

I confess it wasn't pleasant to see Brian standing outside Helen's house in the early hours, it was like he wanted to feel her presence beyond the bricks. The orange sulphur of the street lamp powdered his shoulders as he watched the dark house. 'D'you want me to bring you a hot drink?' I felt like shouting. He'd be there for ages, but there was no movement behind the curtains and eventually he'd walk slowly away toward the park. I thought about trying again, you know, baking another cake and taking it over, but the thought was fleeting and the flour and fruit stayed in the cupboard. The damp started to creep up the walls of Brian's house, his Renault disappeared, I thought he must have gone away to recover, perhaps to Wakefield where he had a sister. Helen had decided which side her bread was buttered, she and Jim could be seen out walking, hand in hand, rather stiffly. When a month had past I asked Flora, his next door neighbour, if she had heard anything and she told me his car had been found on the ferry from Dover to Calais. A few weeks later I heard on the radio that a body had been washed up near Bologne.

It comes on me at the oddest times, when I'm sweeping the yard or peeling potatoes, I get a picture of churning water taking him down through the purple depths. His eyes are always open, in a wide cold stare, gawping at the fish as they swim past his face, his mouth in a huge 'Oh', as he consumes the whole salty ocean. The funny thing is he never floats to the silt, where he could rest in the soft greyness, he just keeps spinning away.

Helen and Jim moved on, out to the country apparently. They didn't say goodbye. There's a young family in Brian's house, they've put a porch on the front and replaced the windows, there's a hanging basket of geraniums out the front.

I try to keep busy. Here's the councillor now.

Gareth J Mews

Gareth is a perpetually travelling, piss taking, self parodying, film geek and cricket fanatic.
He's a proper Northern bloke who's rarely serious
and never 100% joking. He writes about a world
that makes him laugh and despair in equal measure. A chemically fuelled past has injected him
with inspiration but robbed him of brain cells. In
fact bollocks to Frank, talk to him.

Over Front

Trout opened his eyes and groaned, 'Fuck me, what just happened?'

There was no one there to answer him. His mouth was warm and tasted of iron. He rolled around the thick goo with his tongue and spat it out. The red viscous globule escaped his mouth and dripped backwards over his forehead and into his hair. He looked around, it was pretty black but the shadows were starting to form into shapes; grass, rear view mirror, broken glass. He closed his eyes again - that sounds like running water and what the fuck is cutting into my neck? His thoughts weren't all there but they were coming back. He rubbed his face; his hands were like industrial sandpaper with shards of glass embedded in them.

It was coming back. They were in the car. They'd left Burney's party after Lloyd had a barney with Sarah and they were pissed. Not drunk, not over the limit, not a bit worse for wear but well and truly rat-arsed, donnered, trollied. Lloyd had been out back arguing with Sarah when he came storming through, grabbed Trout and pulled him away from young Marie, who always looked dirty - especially so tonight, and off to the car. Lloyd was fuming and Trout didn't argue. He never argued with his much bigger mate, he just followed in his wake, enjoying the ride. The more Lloyd talked the faster he drove.

'That fucking bitch talk to me like that? Like that? Fucking slag! Fucking bitch!' Louder, faster, faster, louder, faster, faster. Trout opened the glove compartment to take his box out. Lloyd was driving fast but the road was straight. Skin up.

And that was it. Now he was here, upside down and getting cold. Where was fucking Lloyd?

Lloyd was gone. Off. He wasn't hanging around to see if
anyone saw his little shunt, he wasn't hanging around to see
what happened to Trout. He'd run about a mile before he
came to a standstill. Lloyd was out of breath, his heart was
racing and he couldn't go on. Heaving air into his lungs, he
fell to his knees behind a stone wall.

'Fuck fuck fuck fuck fuck.' Thoughts and emotions pinballed
round his head, not one coming to the surface. Fear, hatred,
remorse, vindication, fear, lust, fear, betrayal. He let the cold
heavy object slip through his fingers, took a battered cigarette out of his pocket, lit it up, inhaled and began to weep
uncontrollably.

They'd been drinking in the park earlier that afternoon when
Lloyd had shown Trout the gun. He took it from his inside
pocket, it had hanky around it. He laid it on the grass and
slowly unwrapped it. Trout gasped as the content of the parcel was revealed.

'Fucking hell where did you get that?' Trout's eyes were like
saucers.

'You know those Kosovans that hang around Leister Street?'

'Off them? They're fucking mental.'

'No you soft tart. It was all kicking off with them and the
Somalis round African Corner the other night and I was just
kinda watching from inside Burger Jim.'

'By yourself, what were you up to?'

'Never mind. So anyway, there's a few handbags going on,
you know, pushing, shoving, pointing and this and that but
nothing too harsh. And then that big fucker who always
wears a trench coat, even in the summer, you know, the one
that looks like a burns victim.'

97

'Anton?'

'Yeah, him. Well he pulls out this gun and points it at that skinny bloke with all the gold teeth.'

'Fuck off did he, we'd all have heard about that.'

'He fucking did! You calling me a liar?' Lloyd hissed at his smaller friend.

'Alright, chill out. Come on then, what happened?'

'Well he pulled the gun and nothing happened. Just silence. Like everything just stopped. Then all of a sudden, this rock comes out of nowhere and smashes him in the side of the head and he goes down like a sack of shit and they all pulled guns out.'

'And it all kicked off?'

'No. These blokes are soldiers mate. They take no shit but they know when to save face. They all slowly backed away and disappeared.'

Trout was using his index finger to gently push the gun around in the grass.

'What a fucking shit story.'

'Here, fuck you. I'm getting to the good bit.' Lloyd took the gun and carefully put it on the ground under his armpit. 'So I finish my chips and walk over to where the set-to was going on, the place was like a ghost town. And then I catch my foot on the rock that downed Anton and I half stumble. And there on the ground, right in front of me is this fucking gun.'

'And you swiped it?'

'And I swiped it.' Lloyd had a triumphant glint in his eye.

'What the fuck do you want with a gun mate?'

'Protection.'

'You watch too many films man.'

'Bollocks. At least I know to take the safety off before I pull the trigger, unlike that big numb kraut.'

'He's Kosovan.'

'Whatever.'

Trout came too again; he was thirsty.

'There should be some beer on the back seat.' He thought. 'But where it is now I'm upside down though...'

He decided to try and take off the seatbelt maybe he'd get on better the right way up. He might get away before the busies turn up. But they'd crashed way out in the sticks. The busies don't come out to places like this, they let them take care of themselves. He reached towards his waist and found his clothes wringing wet.

'I've fucking pissed myself, great.' He eventually found the seatbelt button and pressed.

A searing pain coursed up Trout's spine, drilling through his sinuses and wrenching his shoulders back. It came from his belly. Trout lay, half folded up against the roof of the car with a feeling of ruin in his gut. It was then that he realised that he couldn't move his legs. They'd stolen the car the night before. There was never anything to do on a Thursday night since the youth club got closed down. It wasn't all that when it was going but at least it was something to do. The pool table had a lean on it, there was no chalk and there were only four darts for the dartboard. The thing was they could go there and chill out. Like hanging round at a mates place without the hassle from parents. They gave Lottie and Amy - the girls who ran it - a fair bit of stick but they were good girls. They got them fags and sometimes drink when they wanted it but usually Trout and Lloyd just turned up stoned after a few buckets in Lloyd's dad's garage and giggled all night. But after that night when they had a huge snowball fight outside, the neighbours complained to the police and the council had the place closed down. Apparently they caused too much trouble and distress for the local community. So what did they do now on a Thursday? Trout would go round Lloyd's dad's garage, they'd smoke a few buckets and go steal a car. Trouble and distress for the local community.

So anyway, they never stole anything fancy. They weren't even proper car thieves. Trout's brother had told him how to hotwire a car years ago, the thing was though that he'd never told him how to get into the car in the first place. So Trout and Lloyd's grand theft auto was based around wandering about until they spotted a car in a dark spot, that was old enough not to have anything as new fangled as an immobiliser or alarm and throwing a brick through the window. Trout would hot wire it then Lloyd would shove him into the passenger seat and race the car to the nearest open space. He would then go through his full but limited repertoire of stalled handbrake turns, half donuts and crunchy gear changes. They would generally tip the car into the canal when they got bored. Or sometimes they would just set light to it, although only if they were a bit more sober. A burning car tends to attract attention and attention tends to mean you have to run. But this time they'd kept the car. This car was different, it belonged to that twat who always complained about them at youth club and now it was theirs.

Burney was a rich kid whose uncle had a farm in the sticks. He was a spoilt bastard and was actually allowed to have par-

ties at the farm when his uncle was away. Trout and Lloyd
would normally have nothing to do with the cunt but Lloyd's
girl, Sarah, was going and he was the protective type. Fuck
knows why. Only last night after parking their new car up at
the back of the hospital, they'd been round Mandy's place
where the pair of them knew they could get it on tap, Lloyd
was shagging her all night while Sarah was no doubt wondering why he wasn't replying to her texts. So anyway, Lloyd
was convinced that Burney was trying to give Sarah one and
he was fizzing. No-one could step on Lloyds territory even
though he could dip his wick wherever and whenever he
wanted. To be fair Burney probably was trying to get into
Sarah but she doted on Lloyd so much she wouldn't even
consider it. Daft cow. But they were bored of dossing
around in the bandstand, smoking spliffs and intimidating
the old women, besides, it was getting cold and there was
fuck all else to do. And if Lloyd didn't shut up about how he
was going to take Burney's head off then Trout was going to
pick up that gun and shoot himself to get some peace.

'Right, are we gonna go up there and sort this cunt out then?'
Lloyd was already on his feet.

'We'll go up there mate but for fucks sake, get shot of that
gun first.'

'What are you, fuckin' pussy or something?'

'Whatever mate but you're not gonna shoot him.' They were
heading through the hospital grounds with their new car
parked up in the leafy lane out the back.

'Scare the living fuck out of him though won't it? He'll think
twice about knobbing my lass again.' They jumped over the
fence; the car was still there.

'Listen mate, don't fuck on. When we get there just leave the
gun in the car. Give him a kicking, fair enough but if you

shoot him, you're fucked.' Trout was getting worried; the last place he wanted to be was prison.

'Alright, we'll leave it in the fucking car, dad.' Lloyd leaned over and put the gun in the glove box.

Trout left the glove box door open and used it as a shelf to skin up on.

'We'll have to swing round by Jassi's and pick up some cans. Jassi was the only bloke who sold alcohol to minors now.

Trout was chatting to Marie. Or rather Marie was droning on about some film that she'd been to see and Trout was staring at her cleavage. Burney was upstairs somewhere cleaning himself up after Lloyd had knocked his two front teeth out and Lloyd and Sarah were arguing in the back garden. Trout was about to ask Marie to follow him upstairs when Lloyd came barging through the crowd and grabbed him by the arm.

'There's fuck all going on here mate. Might as well fuck off.'

Trout didn't have time to argue because by that time they were already out the door. Marie would have to wait, mates came first, fucking mates.

The more Lloyd talked the faster he drove. Louder, faster, faster, louder, faster, faster. Trout opened the glove compartment to take his box out. Lloyd hit a pothole and the gun went off. The ear splitting crack and blinding flash made Lloyd career the car off the road, through the wall and over onto the roof. Trout lay crunched up against the roof of the car, soaked in the blood seeping from the bullet wound in his stomach. He was cold and alone as the last of his life escaped in short gasps. At least Lloyd knew how to take the safety off.

<u>S A Tranter</u>

S A Tranter lives in Edinburgh and has had stories published in print magazines in the UK and the US. He's had too many jobs, all of which he hated, but the night shift taxi driver paid the most.

He's No A Paediatrician

Hello night owls, Danny here on 66.6 FM. I hope you're all fine tonight and I've said a wee prayer for you all. Our first caller is Mary from Pilton. Are you there Mary?

Aye, Am here Danny.

And are you okay Mary?

Eh, naw, no really eh.

Oh dear I'm sad to hear that, what seems to be the problem.

It's him, he just got oot the jail.

Who has Mary?

Ma husband, and see before he went away, before they sent him doon likes, he said when he got oot he'd throw acid in ma face. And I've been getting phone calls but nae one answers...Hello, are you still there Danny.

Yes I'm still here Mary. When did he get out of prison dear.

Last week. Am feart, feart he'll come for me and the kids. He's gonnae chuck acid in ma face and melt ma eyes. He says he's gonnae melt ma eyes.

Listen carefully Mary dear; you need to call the police. Call the police and tell them you're being threatened. They'll help you. Before you hang-up one of my wee helpers will give you the number of the Woman's Refuge in Pilton, okay dear?

But he dusnae care aboot the Polis, the Polis are scared ay him eh, he says he's gonnae stab aw the Polis and that he's gonnae get me and the kids. Am feart Danny.

Don't be afraid Mary. What you need to do is...

I've got to go Danny, I can hear the kids greeting and I think there's someone at the door.

Okay Mary. We're all thinking of you and I'll say a wee prayer for you dear. Well that was poor Mary out in Pilton. She's in our thoughts and our prayers. Our next caller is Jean from Wester Hailes.

Are yi there Danny?...Ah cannae hear yi son?

I'm here Jean...Jean you'll have to turn the radio down Jean.

What's that Danny?

TURN THE RADIO DOWN.

Okay Danny son...how yi keeping pal

Oh I'm hanging by a thread Jean, hanging by a thread, how's yourself sweetheart?

No so good Danny, no so good. They've painted BEAST on ma front door son.

Who has Jean?

Them that live here on the scheme Danny, am scared Danny, and am awfy awfy lonely son. What will a dae Danny.

There's no need to be afraid Jean. Jesus loves you and watches over you.

God bless you Danny. But Danny they painted BEAST on ma front door and they said they're gonnae torch me oot. Said they're gonnae set ays on fire Danny. And they post dog dirt through my letter box. I cannae take much more, am seventy nine Danny. And what aboot ma wee Trixie?

Who's Trixie?

Trixies ma dug. Ma per wee dug, I let her oot by herself for her business and she came back with a pole stuck up her backside Danny. It was trailing behind her. Sticking out her rear-end Danny. Help ays Danny. What um a gonnae dae Danny? Will yi say a prayer for me Danny?

Of course I will Jean. It's all going to be okay.

But how is it Danny? How's it gonnae be okay son?

You need to call the Police Jean. Or make contact with Police Community Outreach Workers. I've got their number.

But I'm no wanting their number Danny. They're dirty buggers them. They're aw huvin sex with the young lassies round here. Underage sex Danny. I can see them from ma windae. They take the young lassies intae the bin chutes at the bottom of the flats. I need oot ay the scheme Danny. Am no gonnae make it son. I've got nae chance. Danny I need oot ay the scheme. They paint BEAST on ma door now but ma son's in the jail. But he was innocent. Ma son wouldnae do a thing like that. No ma laddie, I ken fine well he wouldnae, no ma laddie. He wis always a good wee laddie. He's no a pediatrician. Danny help ays. Help ays son. They're painting BEAST on ma door. Gonnae set fire tae me. And what aboot Trixie...

I'll say a prayer for you Jean.

BUT DANNY. HELP AYS. THEY'RE GONNAE SET FIRE TAE AYS.

God bless you Jean. Well that was Jean out in Wester Hailes. She's in our thoughts and our love goes out to her. Now the next caller is Vince from Gilmerton.

Awright Danny pal. How yi dain mate?

Hanging by a thread Vince, hanging by a thread. What can I do for you son, how can I help you? Remember Jesus loves you.

It's more what I kin dae for you Danny. What I kin dae for you and your callers.

I don't quite understand Vince.

I'm getting a squad ay boys together. And we're gonnae get thum Danny. The bible says an eye fur an eye.

But Vince it also says, love thy neighbour and turn the other cheek.

I'm no bothered aboot aw that shite. You've had two callers on your radio show terrified in their ain hooses. Their ain buckn hooses mind. I mean aye, awright, Jeans laddie wis a BEAST we aw ken that. But he's in the jail now. But there's others oot there Danny. They're still oot there. But so am I. I'm oot there as well, and vengeance is mine sayith the Lord. Jean's per wee dug with a pole rammed up its erse. Sick Danny sick. But am gonnae get a squad ay boys together and tooled up. Aw these sucking scum, am going after them all. Vengeance is mine sayith the Lord. And another thing...

Ah we seem to have lost Vince there. I'll say a prayer for him. Now we have a Vera on the line. Vera from Gracemount.

Danny I'd just like to say that I love everyone, cos everyone's got problems Danny, how you doin by the way Danny, am no drunk mind...

Hanging by a thread Vera and how are you?

Hanging by a tack Danny, did you like that one Danny; hang-

ing by a tack...you still there Danny? No by a thread like what
you say, but by a tack Danny, hanging by a tack. I love you
Danny. I love everyone. I've got problems Danny, and so
have you eh Danny. Am no drunk Danny, Ah dinnae drink
Danny. Ah do have problems Danny. Health problems, no
sex problems though. I've no had sex problems since ma man
died, but I've got diabetes ken? I was up that hospital and
they did tests. I was awfy embarrassed Danny she asked for a
urine sample and a stool sample. And Danny I thought to
myself, what does she want ma stools fur? How's that gonnae
help so ah says to her, well aye okay hen, but you'll need to
send an ambulance for me and the stool cos am no strong
enough to be carrying furniture on the bus. That's when she
told me she wanted to see one of ma SHITS Danny. Am no
drunk Danny. See the other day I was walking ma dog and
see ma balance Danny its away to pot so it is. I fell over intae
this man'ts garden he was awfy angry Danny. But I've no
touched a drop Danny. They've closed the bingo doon Danny.

Oh Vera I'm so sorry for your troubles. Why not come down
to the Church we do bingo on a Wednesday; seven till nine.

We'll we're off for a commercial now. But stay tuned to 66.6
FM. Jesus loves you. See you in five.

*****

Listen Vince it's better if you don't call the show again.

Nae bother Danny. You got that list?

Yes I've got the list.

Vengeance is mine sayith the Lord.

God bless you my son.

Tony & Tula Tew

Tony & Tula have just had their debut novel 'When The Tide Comes In' published and are now working on the sequel. Between them they have forty years experience working with people with 'challenging behaviour' and mental health problems. They thought they had 'seen it all' until they read the stories in 'Radgepacket' and are happy to offer their services free of charge!

Paradise Found

I woke up this morning feeling rather good about myself - maybe I was even feeling a little smug. After years of working non-stop on the daily grind, I finally have the life I think I deserve. In fact, up until now, I can honestly say that I've never lost a days work in my life through sickness, unemployment or any other means. There were even times when I had two jobs running concurrently. It was nothing unusual for me to finish an early shift, come home for a couple of hours, grab some sleep and then head off for a night shift on another job.

I know there are people out there who are jealous of me and there are some who are probably going to work until they drop, who openly begrudge the life I have now carved out for myself. I've never lost any sleep over these losers. I tell myself, 'you only get out of life what you put into it,' and I feel OK when I look at myself in the mirror when I shave - and I always sleep well at night.

While I lie in my bed at night, I often reflect at the irony of it all. Throughout all the years I was working, I always had continuous financial problems - always chasing the next wage packet. It was always a struggle to make ends meet, despite all the extra hours I would put in. There was always something to fork out for and the list seemed endless back then. To pay for all the necessities in life was an achievement in itself. It was rare that there would be anything left over at the end of the month for life's little pleasures. Fees for joining a gym, something I would've loved to have done in my younger years was out of the question. I'd always wanted to become fitter and lead a healthier lifestyle but, it wasn't only the lack of money that prevented me from joining a gym, there was also the lack of motivation. After returning home from work after a hard day, the inspiration to engage in physical activity had waned. Mentally and physically I would be wrecked. By the time I'd returned home, any zest I

110

had woken up in the morning with had evaporated. Even if I could've earned enough I would never have had the time nor the inclination to use the facilities. But, I'd console myself by telling myself that someday, I would have the time - and the money to pursue this lifestyle.

Well here I am today, a little bit older and a little bit wiser, all my dreams come true. I lie here on my bed tired, but it's a different kind of tiredness. I've just completed a weight training session at the new gym, had a swim and finished off with a relaxing half hour in the jacuzzi. After that session, I felt firm and supple. One glance in the mirror - peak fitness achieved.

Lots of people in my social circle take illegal substances to get the kick that I'm feeling right now. I suggest to them that they sort their lives out. The surge of endorphins is still rushing around my head - so who needs artificial stimulants? It's a lifestyle choice. I knew that you couldn't just work all of your adult life then sit and do nothing. If all I intended doing was to sit and watch all the losers on the Jeremy Kyle show, I would've continued working, but I'm too astute to allow that to happen. My father always taught me that an idle mind is a devil's playground. His advice has stayed with me.

During my career I never had the time or the money to commit to a three year Degree course. So now, with the Open University, I'm in my first year as an undergraduate doing a Bachelor of Arts Degree in Classics. I meet up with my course tutor on a regular basis and she gives me all the support I need. In my third year, I'll submit proposals for my Dissertation. It may sound a bit scary, but she'll be there to advise me. Since leaving work, I've also joined some clubs and societies where I've made lots of new friends and since joining the Amateur Dramatics Society on Wednesday evenings, I rub shoulders with politicians, businessmen, solicitors, estate-agents, methodist ministers, catholic priests and people of many different cultures from all around the world. I also joined the golf club. It's good for getting some fresh air into your lungs after a hard day studying indoors - even if the putting green is plagued by snobs.

It had taken me half a lifetime to achieve this good life, only to be shattered by a letter I received in the post this morning. When I opened it, I was dealt a devastating blow. As I sat back in my easy chair and read through it, my worst fears were realised. The letter was from the 'Governor'. He informed me that the Parole Board had taken the decision, without my consent, to release me early on the grounds of exceptionally good conduct. My immediate reaction was to instruct my legal team of probation officers, social worker, solicitors, barristers, anger management counsellors and the Howard League for Penal Reform to protest on my behalf, to the Home Secretary, that my human rights were being infringed upon. However, on discussion with my 'team', I've been informed that I would be entitled to compensation as reimbursement for loss of food and accommodation.

Life is a continuous learning curve isn't it? But if there's one thing I've learnt from this, it's never to be complacent.

Joe Ridgwell

Joe has been widely published on the underground scene and descriptions of him range from 'the hard man of British writing', 'a talented sonofabitch', to a 'literary thug genius'. He thinks we are seeing the decline of western civilization and relishes the prospect of imminent doom. Fight fire with fire, he says, keep searching for the lost elation and load the literary guns!

<u>The Orgasmatron</u>

Leon and George were in a London bar. It was Tuesday evening, and a very dead Tuesday evening at that. The bar staff looked bored, Leon and George looked bored, and one elderly guy plotted up in a darkened corner, might've been dead.

George turned to Leon,

'Don't you think modern life is getting to be like that Woody Allen film?'

Leon took a miniscule sip of his beer and pulled a face, 'This beer tastes like piss.'

George looked at Leon's beer, 'That beer looks like piss.'

Leon signalled to the bartender and ordered two new pints.

'A geezer can only nurse a beer so long before it becomes undrinkable,' reflected George.

Leon took a healthy swig from his fresh pint,' Which Woody Allen film?'

'What?'

'Which Woody Allen film is life now reflecting?'

'Is it art imitating life, or life imitating art?'

'Huh?'

'Forget it, it's Sleeper.'

'Sleeper?'

'The one where Woody Allen's character awakens in the future.'

'I know that one, I've seen it five or six times, a very funny film.'

'Back then Allen was at his peak and most of his films were funny, unlike now, when all of his films are incredibly unfunny.'

'Shit, how does that shit work?'

'What shit?'

'Going from funny to unfunny?'

'I reckon there's a limit to any man's talent. After a while they just run out of ideas.'

'Like musicians?'

'Yep, and painters and writers.'

'Writers?'

'Especially writers.'

'What about geniuses?'

'Genius lasts a little longer, but not much.'

'That's kinda depressing George.'

'No it's not, what's depressing is that most people don't have any ideas at all.'

George and Leon took a reflective sip from their respective pints.

'Take this bird I met at the train station,' said George.

'What happened?'

'We get the same train each morning.'

'And?'

'And we spend a few weeks exchanging glances.'

'Yeah?'

'Yeah, and when we finally get to speak, she thought I wanted to kill her.'

'You do have a thuggish disposition.'

'I do?'

'I just didn't want to tell you.'

'Thanks friend.'

'Anyway, one night after work, we bump into each other on the way home. I've had a few jars and just blurt it out.'

'Blurt what out?'

'Is she single, does she want to go for a drink, the usual crap?'

'Any luck?'

George put his pint down on the bar and assumed a shocked expression, 'A man with my charms does not need luck.'

'So you pulled?'

'We exchanged numbers and began texting each other, but that's as far as it went.'

'Huh?'

'Turns out the tart has a boyfriend.'

'What has that got to do with Woody Allen?'

'Remember the Orgasmatron?'

Leon smiled fondly, 'Yeah, I always wanted one of those machines.'

'Understandable, but get this, the freaky bitch only wanted me for text sex.'

'Text sex?'

'The boyfriend works nights and she texts me when he's on the job.'

'Ha, ha, and then you get on the job?'

'It might seem unbelievable, but those texts were enough to get me harder than granite,'

'Why didn't she just call?'

'People no longer want intimate contact; they don't even want to speak to each other. This girl just kept sending texts, some of the filthiest language I'd ever read, until she got her rocks off.'

'Did you get your rocks off?'

'Fucking right I did, and it was a good deal easier than a full blown affair.'

'I can imagine?'

At this point George and Leon went outside for a cigarette. It was cold outside, so they smoked the fags in world record time and then beat a hasty retreat.

'Then there's the internet and social networking,' said George once they were back in the warmth of the bar.

Leon rubbed his hands together, 'What about 'em?'

'They masquerade as sites for artists, musicians, young professionals etc. In reality everyone's talking dirty, titillating the shit out of each other.'

'That reminds me, I've got to invest in a laptop,' mumbled Leon.

George ordered two more beers, 'And don't forget a webcam.'

'A webcam?'

'More titillation. This Aussie bird gets in touch with me via Facebook, wants to chat, email. Remember she's living on the other side of the world, but with today's technology we're able to communicate in seconds. Then she asks if I've got a webcam, wants to see what I look like.'

'So what do you do?'

'I've seen the girl's pictures, blonde, nice tits. I invest in a webcam. Next thing I know we're looking at each other through a fucking screen.'

Leon looked up from his beer in disbelief, 'Shit.'

'I can see her, but I don't actually have to be in the same room as her, or talk to her afterwards, a no-brainer. She's wearing pink knickers, frilly satin things. I get the horn straight away.'

'You mean she stripped?'

'She did anything I fucking asked, no questions. After ten minutes she was butt naked, fingering her twat and playing with her nipples pure porno style.'

'And what did you do?'

'I bashed one out, what d'ya think I fucking did?'

Leon let out a low whistle and swigged from his pint, 'And this was all free?'

'Gratis.'

'But surely that sort of interaction will never replace physical sex?'

George rubbed his six-day old stubble and patted his beer belly thoughtfully, 'Maybe, maybe not, but it sure is less complicated and less risky. As far as I can see we are now living in a society where convenience is the number one priority.'

'You said it,' said Leon.

'I mean, it's early days, but given enough time I don't think people will bother with relationships in the future, too much hassle, and ultimately way too incon-fucking-venient.'

After this convo the two friends remained silent, each one reflecting on the implications of what had been discussed. As they did two women walked into the bar. They were mid-to-late thirties, similar in age to George and Leon, and looked to be up for a little action. Leon was the first to notice.

'Did you check those two out?' He asked.

George raised his beer and gave the women a quick once over, 'Mingers,' he said hastily.

The women ordered drinks and remained at the bar. Every now and again they looked over and smiled.

'Shit, I think we've made a connection,' hissed Leon.

George downed the rest of his pint, 'Nah, fuck 'em. Too much like hard work, bound to be a couple prick teases.'

Leon swigged the last of his pint, 'The night is young George.'

George thought about his nine o'clock webcam date with a sexy girl from Thailand. She'd already shown him her tits and he reckoned tonight she'd get her rat out, 'Listen I've gotta be going.'

The woman continued to smile, one even waved.

'Gotta be going?' protested Leon.

George shot the two women another glance and then put on his jacket,

'You coming or what?'

Leon stood up and reluctantly followed suit. Maybe his friend was right, maybe people were losing the ability to interact with each other, but on the other hand, maybe it was just George?

Outside it was still a dead Tuesday evening, which in Leon's mind had just become a little deader.

David Ciurlionis

David is the greatest ever New Zealand/Lithuanian writer working in the English Language (he checked Google and there aren't any others). He recycles and always throws his cigarette butts in the bin. He enjoys watching television and jumping on his bed.

Tube

The tube was late today
Twelve minute wait
8.41
Northern Line
Monday morning
Chaos
I was spewing hate
At everyone
You useless Cunt
My eyes said to the platform attendant
Aggressively wide open
Touch me again you old bitch and see what happens
Said my violently pursed lips
I mouthed 'Fuck you' at the driver as the train went past
I was livid with these people
Where was I so desperate to go?
Work?
To sit in a chair
For nine hours
With no lunch break
On a thirty degree day
Wearing a suit and tie
And balance sales ledgers for a mid sized private equity firm

I can see where my hate comes from.

Bus

Bus
Evening Commute
Hard Day
Suddenly
Dizzie Rascal
Fucken Loud
On a Cell Phone
Five seats back
Teenager
Sixteen years old
Trying to look hard
I'm twenty six
And am shattered.

My free Paper
Has the same headline
It always has
Eighteen yr old stabbed
Man stabbed
Stabbed, stabbed, stabbed
I should get up
'Turn off your music'
'We don't all want to hear it'
'Have you heard of headphones'
'You inconsiderate little cunt'
Maybe leave out the cunt bit.

I reckon
The chances of me getting stabbed
Or hurt
are very small
But we will never know
Cause I sit there and don't say shit
Cause I'm scared I'll get stabbed.

Nick Quantrill

Nick lives and works in Hull (never mind eh...) When not worrying about the fortunes of Hull City AFC or where his next coffee's coming from, he's hard at work on his novel, 'Broken Dreams', which will appear via Caffeine Nights Publishing in 2009. He can be found at www.hullcrimefiction.co.uk

Party Politics

'Why me? I asked.

'Because you're a Private Investigator. You're discreet. If the film gets into the wrong hands, it would cause me huge embarrassment. I'm sure you can see that, can't you, Mr Geraghty?'

Peter Snow smiled at me. A politician's smile. He was wearing a local politician's suit - cheap, but not too cheap. Well groomed. Just enough to say there was something about him, but not enough to intimidate. I told him to call me Joe.

'What does your wife say about it?'

Snow looked away from me. 'I haven't told her.'

I nodded. The business had bills to pay. Private Investigation isn't the easiest way to make a living in Hull.

'I was naive, Joe.' He flashed me his smile again. 'But we've put it behind me. I've had to. The election is coming up and I've spent months campaigning around the city. I can't let it go now. I've put years in working for this chance. I've sat on all the small time committees and attended countless soul destroying meetings about petty local issues. I deserve a shot at leading the city.'

He removed a piece of paper from his pocket and passed it over to me. 'This is the toe-rag who's got the tape.'

I looked at the address and tried not to show my disappointment; one of the few remaining tower blocks on one of the city's most notorious council estates.

'I'm told this man runs some sort of pornography empire from his flat.'

I shrugged. 'All you need is a DVD recorder and a load of
blanks.' You could be selling them around the markets within
hours. Plenty of them around the place and nobody was
going to stop you. It sounded like the kind of minor scandal
which would tip things in your opponent's favour. The city
went to the polls next week and it's a two horse race between
Labour and the Lib Dems. If Snow's party won, he'd be the
leader of the council. Even in the provincial North, it wasn't
to be sniffed at.

'You'll get it back for me?' he asked, opening his chequebook.

'I can pay you £500 now for your trouble and I'll pay the
same again when you bring the tape back. Obviously I'll pay
whatever it costs to buy it back.'

I picked the cheque up, read it and put it in my drawer. Don,
my partner, was out doing our bread and butter work, serv-
ing warrants and tracking down court witnesses. It paid, but
it didn't pay £1,000 for a couple of hours work. I quite liked
Snow's opponent, Jeremy Brown, but not so much I wouldn't
take the job. Brown had been round the block a few times,
but Snow was younger. Maybe he was the future of the city,
the kind of man the place needed. I probably wasn't the best
to judge.

He stood up and offered his hand. 'Thanks for your help and
discretion. You're making a genuine difference to my campaign. I won't forget it. I trust I can count on your vote next
week?'

*****

I looked at the tower block and winced. The flat was on the
fourteenth floor and I bet the lift was out of order. Avoiding
the dog shit on the ground and the stares from the local
hoodies, I headed up the stairs. Knocking on the door, I tried
to block the smell of disinfectant and piss from my nose.

The door opened. 'Yeah?'

The man was in his mid-forties, the same age as Snow, but he looked a lot older. And less well groomed.

I checked the name Snow had given me. 'Brian Wood?'

'Who's asking?'

'A friend told me about you. I want to buy a film.'

He gave me a toothy grin and nodded me in. 'I cater for all tastes, me. Satisfaction guaranteed or your money back.' He laughed and led me into the front room.

'You're not the filth, are you?'

'No.'

'Didn't think so. You don't look the part.'

I didn't want to sit down; the couch was filthy and I'd have to remove the empty beer cans first. A large flat-screen television dominated the room, no expense spared. A top of the range camcorder was on the floor.

'If you've come about the new one, it's not in yet,' he said.

'No worries.'

'The things people will do for twenty quid's phone credit.' Wood said, shaking his head. He disappeared out of the room and brought back a box of DVDs for me to look through. 'Loads of good stuff in there.' He picked out a few titles and passed them over to me. 'Lots of local stuff, too, if you're into that kind of thing. Did most of them myself. There's some right mucky cows around here.'

I put the box down and told him which film I wanted. 'I want to buy it off you. Master-tape, stock, the whole lot.'

'I know the one you mean.' Wood lit a cigarette and stared at me. 'The politician bloke.'

'Right.'

He walked me over to the window. The view from the fourteenth floor was spectacular. 'It's a good film, that one. Took me a lot of time and money to get it.'

'I'm sure it did.'

'I've got overheads.'

'Haven't we all.' I watched him take one last drag of his cigarette. 'I'll give you £400.'

'He must want it back pretty bad.'

'We all do things we regret.'

'There's a credit crunch on, Joe.'

It wasn't my money. '£500 is the best I can do.'

Wood took his time before turning to face me. 'I suppose he can have it if he wants it that bad.'

Five minutes later, and after refusing a can of lager to seal the deal, I was out of the flat and heading down the stairs towards my car. Fresh air had never felt so good on my face. The same group of teenagers I'd seen on my way into the flats were stood around the stairwell, kicking a football between them.

One of them stepped forwards. 'Got a cig?'

I shook my head. 'Sorry.'

'Best give us the money to buy some, then.'

The rest of the gang moved towards me, kicking the ball at me. Fucks sake. I'd played professional rugby league. I could handle myself if I needed to. Then it all turned dark.

*****

Sarah threw the newspaper on my desk.

'How's the head?' she asked.

'Still there.' I had seven stitches in the back of my head, a thumping headache and a black eye to show for my troubles. What I didn't have was the DVD.

The newspaper had landed sports page up. A clear sign I should read it.

'Front page,' Sarah said, standing over me.

I turned it over and read the headline. My headache intensified. I swallowed a couple more paracetamol and stood up, looking for my coat. 'I'll see you later.'

I sat down next to Snow and showed him the newspaper. The pub was almost empty, and being in the city centre, it only had a smattering of regulars propping up the bar. It was quiet and private.

'We could have done this at my office,' he said to me.

I shook my head. 'Here's fine. I think you owe me an explanation.' I put my mobile on the table and sat back.

Snow sighed and passed me over an envelope.

'More than we agreed,' I said, counting £1,500.

'For your troubles.'

'You didn't tell me the truth.'

'Technically not, maybe. The point is still the same, though. I need to win this election.'

I pointed at the news headline. 'You've made me look stupid.'

Underneath the headline, the story explained how I'd been attacked outside the tower block. Conveniently found by a passing Samaritan, I'd been taken to the hospital where the DVD had been found on me.

'Remarkable that the DVD made its way to the paper. Imagine my surprise when I learnt you weren't on it.'

'I've made you look like a hero,' Snow said, 'and I made sure you came to no harm.'

I took a deep breath and ignored what he'd just said. I pointed to the headline. 'Jeremy Brown's the star of the DVD.' The woman on it probably wasn't even born when Brown had married his wife.

'I have to win this election.'

'Why shouldn't Brown win it?'

He leant forward. 'I told you. I've spent my whole life working for this.'

'And you found out about this DVD?'

Snow nodded.

'But you couldn't just buy a copy and leak it, could you?' I thought back to meeting Brian Wood. He knew my name. 'I was expected at the tower block wasn't I?'

Snow nodded again.

'You set me up.'

'No harm done, though.'

'Apart from my head.'

'It'll heal. Once I win next week, who knows? I might well need your services again.'

I shook my head, not quite believing how far he'd gone. 'It had to be a story, didn't it?' And I was the story. 'If I was found with the DVD, it doesn't look like a smear on Brown, does it? Your story's beyond reproach. The press contact Brown who denies any knowledge of knowing me, as he would, but given he has no credibility, it's easy to imply he sent me to retrieve the film. You must have made some good friends in the media.'

Snow at least had the decency to not look me in the eye. 'That's pretty much it.'

'And you clean up when the city votes next week?'

'The end justifies the means.'

I put the envelope in my pocket. The bills still needed paying. 'You want my vote?'

Snow nodded. 'I'm the best choice for this city.

I shook my head and stood up. I liked Brown and thought he'd do a decent job of getting the city back on its feet.

Whether he could put this behind him, I didn't know. It wasn't my decision to make. I picked my mobile up off the table and pressed stop on the recorder. I nodded to Don, who sat a few feet away from us, nursing a pint.

'Did you get a good shot of me counting the money?' I asked him. Don's mobile had a state of the art camera built into it. 'Certainly did. How's the sound on your phone?'

'Crystal clear.' I had to make sure Snow's role in this came out. Sometimes it pays to have the latest gadgets in this job.

I turned back to Snow and smiled. 'I think we can say you've not got my vote, but I'll see what I can do for your campaign.'

This Issue...

Daniel Mayhew

'Dead Mans Suit'

The Radgepacket Tapes

Competition Time

Win a signed copy of

'Life And How To Live It'

Dead Man's Suit

Fame is a curious thing. I've gone through sixty eight years without so much of a hint of it. I never wanted attention, never courted it, but all of a sudden I am a genuine celebrity. I have quite a following now and it's growing all the time. My fame is a strange kind in that it's second-hand; it's someone else's fame that has landed on my doorstep.I sit here on a Saturday evening in the dark save for the flickering of the telly. It's brutally cold out and I'm glad to be inside. There's a singing contest on the telly and I'm slumped into my old set-tee (well away from the window just in case). A contestant is saying that if she couldn't sing, she would rather be dead. She just wants the public to vote for her. She says she wants to give her family a better life. She looks tearful. She starts singing; it's a big booming song about her heart. It's not quite my thing but she clearly has talent. I guess it's not bad.

The phone rings and it takes me by surprise. I rush up the hall way to the kitchen, flicking the lights on. It's Judith. She asks me if they've been round yet and I tell her they haven't. I don't tell her about what happened today because I know she'll worry. It's difficult for Judith. She never wanted me to move out but I insisted on it. When the cancer went and I didn't die as I was supposed to I couldn't go on being cared for could I? She says all this is worse than seeing me go through the chemo and the ops. 'Look after yourself Dad. Phone me if you need me,' she says and I put the phone down and go back to my seat in front of the telly.

I caught one this afternoon. I was washing up, listening to the football on the radio. City had just equalised and I allowed myself a little smile. Then I looked up at the window and through the condensation I saw a figure in the yard. I slipped the marigolds off and quietly opened the back door. And there he was, a little lad in one of those hooded tops and tracksuit bottoms, spray-painting the wall. I stepped out and asked him what he was doing. He jolted as if shot at, and fixed me with wild eyes. He turned quickly and considered the back gate, but I grabbed him. He struggled wildly, shouting for his mates who were nowhere to be seen. I dragged him inside, locked the back door and sat him down at the kitchen table. 'Now then,' I said, but he didn't reply. He was mute but breathing heavily. Sweating.

On the telly the judges are giving their verdicts. Three of them like the singer, but one of them doesn't. He looks really unhappy this man, I feel sorry for him. Maybe he needs a bout of stomach cancer to put things into perspective. Then it's another contestant's turn. They start showing film of him with his family. His brother is horrifically disabled, cerebal palsy, the big one. Like the last contestant, he wants a better life for his family. He wants to live his dream he says and fill stadiums. There are more tears.

Being told you're going to die gets your attention. But not straight away like you might expect. When the doctor came out with it I laughed. 'I feel fine,' I told him, 'You've got the results mixed up.' He seemed ready for this and told me that was impossible. Six months he said. 'Bugger me,' I replied. It was weeks later when the burning grief came, the bruising pounding anger at the injustice of it all. At the prospect of leaving Judith and Tilly.

The lad caught his breath and started to talk. 'Are you going to kill me?' he asked. Poor lad. I told him I wasn't going to kill him. Then he started shouting.

'You sick fucker. You paedo scum. You won't get away with this, my brother knows where I am.' His aggression was alarming.

'Do you want a cup of tea?' I said, as a reflex.

'What?'

'Never mind.'

'Just let me go.'

'No, I want to talk to you.'

He didn't reply. He wouldn't meet my eye. 'What's your name?' I asked.

'Fuck off.' This made me laugh for some reason.

'Why were you in my yard?'

'Fuck off.' He still wouldn't look at me.

'I'm not him you know.'

That made him look at me. 'Yes you are. You fucked and killed those kids.'

Since I was dying Judith suggested I sell up and move in with her. This made sense, and I wanted to spend my last few months with her, my only child. My best friend. She was three months pregnant when I moved in; by this lad who never treated her right and was long gone anyway. And so we got on with things, ploughing through our different conditions. She bloomed and glowed and became more beautiful while the drugs killed every cell in my body, trying to terrorise the tumour from my stomach. Sick doesn't describe it, chemo, and I didn't even have the Full Monty. I was only plugged in for four hours a day but still I withered. But I won't wallow in it. It's quite an experience, killing yourself so you might live. And that's what I did, bit by bit. After Tilly was born we went back to the doctor and he told me I was 'in remission.' Those words. But what was strange was that I felt a bit cheated. By that time quite fine with the idea of dying in my sixties.

'What's your name?' I asked the lad.

'Not telling you.'

'I'm Jim,' I told him.

'No you're not, I know who you are.'

'I look nothing like him. Look at me; I'm about twenty years too old.'

'You've had plastic surgery, my dad told me.'

'What?'

'You've had plastic surgery, a new identity and they've bought you a bloody house. But you're not welcome here, not in this street. You've no right.'

Don't get me wrong, I'm grateful that I survived. It's changed me. I don't see things in the same way anymore. I imagine an ancestor looking back at my life in a thousand years. What would they find out? Birth date, occupation, death date? It strikes me that it doesn't matter. I look at the world, at people, at my tormentors even with curiosity. Judith though, she only has anger. When it was all first kicking off she went up and down the street, Tilly in her arms, knocking on doors. She pleaded with them to stop smashing my windows and spitting at me, but of course they all denied all knowledge. Fair enough. You don't admit to things like that.

It started with a brick through my bedroom window. It seemed strange but not that unusual in this street. But then a few nights later another brick went through the kitchen window. And then they started to gather in the darkness and shout things at me. The police told me there was a rumour that I was him, the man who raped and killed the two little boys down south in the eighties. As with the cancer, I laughed. The police gave me a panic alarm and put CCTV cameras up, but this seemed to confirm to the mob that I was him. The bricks kept coming and at one point I had no window in the house without plywood covering it. It was bloody strange having no light coming in. It's desperate and lonely, like living in a cave, but the plywood stopped the bricks just fine. As the windows were re-glazed, they were quickly de-glazed once more. I got fireworks, dog shit and used tampons through the letter box. And things you wouldn't expect too: half-eaten kebabs, empty fag packets, mud, pornography. I wouldn't let Judith read the hate mail because I knew it would upset her, but I came to find it strangely interesting. How could people hate a stranger this much? And how come people can't spell anymore? 'Fuk u fukked up kiddie fiddler. We r gonna kill ya;' 'You deserve to hang 4 what u did to those kids ya sick fucker;' 'Don't even think of touching our kids you sick beast. Get the fuck out of our city.' Don't get me wrong, I'm not perfect. When I was a lad I believed that immigrants were stealing our jobs. I believed that women should stay in the home. I believed in the death penalty. But then I grew up.

'What if I was him?' I asked the lad. He looked me up and down and in his face I could see his thoughts forming. I studied him; I wanted to understand how he'd got to here. To spray-painting obscenities on my wall. This little lad. Pale faced, shaking. Once upon a time he was a newborn baby boy, people were happy at his birth, watched him grow.

He spoke. 'You fucking are him aren't you?'

This made me feel tired and I sighed. 'Go on then,' I told him. 'Go home.'

I opened the back door and he strutted out. He sneered at me as he left, more confident now. 'You fucking are him,' he said to me. I watched him leave.

There's an ad break on so I go to make myself another cup of tea. It's been quiet for a Saturday, which can be ominous. I'm expecting some kind of fall-out from this afternoon with the lad. The kettle boils but I don't fancy tea anymore. I pour myself two fingers of Bells and get back to my spot on the settee. I know I shouldn't drink whisky; my surgically reduced stomach isn't really up to it. But two fingers gives me a nice glow, and it's all I can tolerate.

On the singing contest they're explaining that one of the contestants is going be voted out. It all seems quite brutal to me but I watch it nonetheless. They string it out and all the contestants are close to tears. It's incredibly cruel. It's the girl who was singing about her heart. She didn't get enough votes. She's out. The other contestants embrace her and she breaks down. I've seen enough.

I finish my whiskey, turn the telly and lights off and head for bed. I brush my teeth, looking at my grizzled face in the mirror. I chuckle at my image, silly old man. I warm a flannel under the tap and wash my face. In my bedroom I change into my pyjamas (the ones Judith got me for my birthday) and slip my body into bed. I lay in the darkness and feel the stillness. I feel good, relaxed and I begin to drift off.
Then I hear familiar voices outside. Chattering and shushing each other. I can't make out the words but I know what's coming. There's a crash downstairs as a window goes through. I don't feel surprise or shock. I feel weary. I'll just deal with it tomorrow.

But now I can smell smoke. And now I see a glow through the crack in my bedroom door. I can hear the fire crackling up the stairs, accelerating up the old carpet. I can see it in my mind, advancing up to the first floor. I feel a gush of heat and the smoke gets thicker and there's nothing I can do. I close my eyes.

The Radgepacket Tapes

Ever been to York? Proper city full of massive blokes and charming young ladies - well that's what my latest interviewee says anyway and frankly, I believe him. Daniel Mayhew, author of the critically acclaimed 'Life And How To Live It' has the look of a stand up comedian, the writing style of Christopher Brookmyre crossed with John King and, most importantly, a broken glass nestling against my throat...that's why I'm agreeing with the York thing...gulp.

So Danny boy, what's going on at the moment?

The weather's awful and I'm worried sick about Spurs. Apart from that I'm writing a short story for a future Radgepacket which I'm really enjoying. It's a cheerful little thing set in the north about celebrity, cancer and angry mobs. I'm also writing my second novel, *'I am Trying to Break Your Heart'*, doing some promotion for *'How Not to Manage'* which was published in November as well as planning the follow up.

You're becoming a bit of an underground cult (I said cult - stop pushing that glass in man...) for your debut novel. Was it a conscious decision to go in the direction you did or did you find that you started writing and just got dragged that way?

My starting point was an idea I had of doing a modern re-telling of John Kennedy Toole's *'A Confederacy of Dunces.'* After a bit of consideration I thought it could work if the Ignatius J Reilly character was a music obsessive rather than a moral philosophy obsessive. Then it kind of evolved into a novel about a band and got further and further away from a re-telling of *'Confederacy'*. In the end it was a grateful nod in the direction of it I think. I very much got dragged in the direction I went in, there was very little conscious planning about what I was doing other than wanting to write the kind of book I wanted to read and thought other people might enjoy.

As it turned out writing a novel about a band was commercial suicide. I found out that in the publishing industry, 'rock novels' as they call them are notorious in that they are normally rubbish and even if they're any good, don't sell any copies. So I unwittingly made things very hard for myself.

As well as the novel have you written anything else we should be looking out for?

Yes, *'How Not to Manage'* which is a satirical management manual that I co-wrote with Adam Kirkman. It's a piss-take of management guides and big business and rubbish managers generally. It's a bit of fun after doing a novel. Someone I know called it a 'toilet book' as a compliment. I think that's pretty spot on.

Who or what would you say was responsible for motivating young Daniel to take up the pen initially?

Hard to say. I remember being about twenty and first reading *'Marabou Stork Nightmares'* by Irvine Welsh and he was writing about things I could relate to rather than 18th century sea captains or whatever and the thought first occurred to me that maybe I could have a crack at this. But for a long time I thought that you had to be a genius to write a novel and had to have done an MA in creative writing or something. It was a good few years later when I actually got the courage to try. I was about twenty seven I think. It was probably a good thing that I waited because if I had written a novel when I was twenty it would have been fairly shit I think.

And this might sound a bit negative but it's honest - I have always been inspired by reading novels which are really bad as it makes me want to do something better. I was about half way through writing *'Life'* and was a bit stuck with it and thinking I was a deluded fool when I for some reason read *'Popcorn'* by Ben Elton which I thought was fucking terrible frankly. And it really inspired me **(We're with you all the way there kidda! Ed)**

It's nigh on impossible for an unknown, particularly someone who writes 'a bit street' like you do, to get a publisher these days - how did you manage it?

That's the first time anyone's said I was 'a bit street.' Thanks very much.

I got a publisher in the same way most writers do by being almost pathologically persistent and getting a bit of luck. It was quite a weird process really. It took about two and half years. I decided that I wouldn't approach any agents until the book was finished but I saw a competition called Lit Idol which was at the London Book Fair in I think 2004. I was living in Australia then.

I sent three chapters and got longlisted which meant I got a bit of publicity and a well-known agent in London said lots of nice things to me and generally strung me along for a few months before wishing me good luck and sending me on my way. It was massively distracting. Then when the book was finished I sent it out to lots and lots of agents and then another agent took it on but nothing happened and I binned him after about a year. And then I read about a new independent publisher, set up by Adam Kirkman who I ended up writing *'How Not to Manage'* with, which was based in York which was handy because I live there and I got in touch with them and we had a few conversations and they eventually went for it.

It was lucky timing because as it was a new publisher they were looking for things to fill their lists then, but already they are full for about two years ahead.

What are you reading at the minute then (apart from Radgepacket obviously)?

I'm reading a novel called *'Start From Here'* by Sean French and its unspeakable bollocks in every way. It's a disgrace.

Recently I read something much better. *'A Fraction of the Whole'* by Steve Toltz. The best thing I've read in a few years actually. It's funny, very intelligent and the characters and set pieces are fantastic. It should have won the Booker.

'Life And How To Live It' charts the trials and tribulations of a band where one member wants to be successful and the other doesn't - how hard was it to write a book about music and avoid loads of obscure in-jokes?

It's not a thing I ever struggled with. I was conscious that some of the references to obscure bands wouldn't mean much to a lot of people, but I used them in that way, to illustrate that the characters really cared about these bands that most people have never heard of. I did at times wonder whether it would alienate people but I thought if it was sincere it would work.

For example I read a lot of North American fiction and don't get some of the cultural references. But I don't put the book down thinking 'I've never heard of that!' If the book has a point to it and is written with sincerity then I trust it and read on.

I always thought of my novel as being about creative guilt and aspiration rather than about a band. The band is just the setting.

Either of the characters based on you?

No. Reilly and Jacob are much more interesting than me. I don't consider myself to be an interesting enough character to carry a book and I'm suspicious of anyone who does.

Reilly in particular is an extreme person and possibly mentally ill but personally I like reading novels about extreme people who are possibly mentally ill. I had the best time writing Reilly, I'm very fond of him. He's a nightmare but is fundamentally a moralist with very strong ideals but what's interesting to me is that isn't feasible to live in the way he does.

What have you lashed all the millions on then - trainers, bling or McDonalds?

I'm not into material things at all. However, the exception to this rule is trainers. I am obsessed with the things and have way too many of them to be able to justify rationally.

We have a number of literary heroes here at BB Towers - who would you say yours were and why?

I read all kinds of things - I'll give most things a go. I'll read anything which I think is sincere. I like the comedy in Jane Austen, Henry James, Oscar Wilde. Shakespeare is an obvious one but it's incredibly powerful writing. John Ford too. Camus.

My favourite novel is 'The Secret History' by Donna Tart. I really admire Roddy Doyle, the way he progressed and got better and better. 'The Commitments' is great but quite raw from a style point of view whereas 'A Star Called Henry' is lyrical really.

I think that in terms of modern story-tellers, I don't think anyone can touch Jimmy McGovern, 'Cracker' was great but

'The Street' was absolutely astounding. I can't believe how good it was. He's definitely a hero.

Writers that are more similar to me that I like - John King, earlier Irvine Welsh, Hunter S Thompson, Kerouac, Palahniuk. *'Fight Club'* is for me is near perfect as a novel. By the way I think William Burroughs was shit. He couldn't write.

'A Clockwork Orange' is so good. Like *'Fight Club'*, the novel is overshadowed by the film to an extent, but it is such a good novel. A huge central subject, brilliant characters, big ideas, humour and Burgess invents a language! Brilliant.

To pick one hero though - George Orwell. Everything he wrote was extraordinary, quite a feat.

A thing I really like about say *'Animal Farm'* and *'1984'* is the brevity. Like *'A Clockwork Orange'* they are not long novels. For me this is very important because it means the power of the books isn't diluted.

I think a lot of modern novels are fifty to a hundred pages too long. And *'1984'* could have been written today. It's timeless.

Any advice you could give the millions of writers and authors out there who never get a sniff of publication?

Just keep writing and keep reading. Read lots of different things and notice what works and what doesn't. And just keep at it and don't be bothered by rejections.

There are a million reasons why your work can get rejected and most of these have nothing to do with the quality of it. Enjoy yourself and write the best stuff you can.

Keep submitting your work far and wide and don't get too hung up on the idea of publication as the goal.

Ever considered abseiling down the Houses of Parliament dressed as Batman to get some publicity?

Do you know what? That has honestly never occurred to me. It's worth a try though.

Do you follow the old adage of 'write what you know' and if so how many bands have you been in?

None. Although I can play the guitar a bit and have done the odd bit of home recording over the years with friends, so I know the basics. I've never done a gig and never been in a recording studio. I know a lot of people in bands though and I'm very into music so I didn't have to do loads of research.

Who would play you in the film of your life?

Heath Ledger could have done it but, you know, I reckon Sacha Baron Cohen would look a bit like me with a wig on. **(Ha ha - Yes he would! Ed)**

And what sort of soundtrack would you like playing?

Where to start? Four Tet and Boards of Canada are nice and cinematic. Burial too. I could go on.

Did you find that you had to change your style or content to get publishers interested in you initially?

I probably should have done but absolutely no, I never did that and never would. I'd rather starve than write a novel that wasn't what I wanted it to be or I wasn't absolutely happy to put my name to.

And the title of your books being genuine song titles - how did that happen?

I've always loved '*Life and How to Live It*' by REM as a song title. As an idea you couldn't get any bigger. The idea that a song or a book or anything could tell you this tickles me. It also fits the book because in essence this is exactly what every character in the book is wrestling with.

I got an email from a guy who'd read the book who told me about the story behind the song. I had no idea about it so it was great. Apparently there was a guy somewhere in America who was a recluse who never left his home. Just because he was a bit bored of his house he split it into two halves so he had two homes. Anyway he grew old and died and the authorities discovered this unusual existence he'd been living.

 The house was full of things he'd hoarded. In a cupboard they found a big pile of books, hundreds of copies of a book he had written and had presumably had printed, delivered but had never left his house. The book was called '*Life and How to Live It.*' If you've read my book you will know that this is ever so slightly spooky.

The title of the next novel, 'I Am Trying To Break Your Heart' is a Wilco song. Similar story really - I just like the title.

Does that lead to any copyright problems?

No not at all. You can use song titles with no problem. Book titles are a bit different as you can get accused of 'passing off' your work as something that it's not. The chapter titles in '*Life and How to Live it*' are all song titles too. A brilliant thing that's happened since the book came out is that I've heard from some of the people that wrote these songs. None of them told me they had a problem with me using their titles, I think they quite liked it.

And finally, but most importantly, assuming that your books become massive, multi million pound film productions is there any chance you might need a fifteen stone shaven headed Geordie to play a lead role and get all the girls??

Definitely. I'd insist on it. You could play Madeleine. I'd plead artistic integrity and have a tantrum if necessary.

The Radgepacket team and all at Byker Books would like to take this opportunity to thank Daniel for giving us his time so freely during this interview. We obviously wish him continued success with his writing career and suggest you have a gander at his work as it's canny good.

We would also like to confirm that the glass at the throat thing was just a bit of nonsense we made up...honest it was...put it down now Danny eh...Aaaiiyaahh!

Competition Time

Here we are again then kids, the end of another Radgepacket. Whatever shall we do you ask? How shall we get a fix of top quality British fiction? How on earth can we wait until the next Radge hits the streets? You can't just cut us off like this you heartless Northern gets - we've become addicted to the wit and the grit you purvey!

Well worry not, help is at hand because, young Mr Mayhew stupidly turned his back when we were interviewing him and we managed to swipe five signed copies of his critically acclaimed book *'Life And How To Live It'* that were destined for somewhere else (bloody *Zoo* or *Nuts* probably!)

All you have to do to win a copy of this top book and impress all your friends is email :-

ed@bykerbooks.co.uk

with your address and the answer to this question.

Which football team does Daniel support?

The closing date for this competition is 30th October 2009.

Please enter '**Radgepacket 3 Competition**' as the subject line of your email, all those that fail to do so disqualify themselves instantly.

Winners will be chosen at random and notified by email. The editor's decision is final and no correspondence will be entered into if you don't win- so don't bother.

Right, what are you waiting for? Get on it.

Coming soon...from Byker Books

I'M RIVELINO

Andy Rivers

'When you think of them in a football sense you think of 'little Rotherham ...oh the romance of the cup.' Well all I could see was fifteen stone, pie eating nutters covered in tattoos and no matter how much aftershave they'd slapped on there'd be no f**king romance going on there I can tell you...!'

Thanks to a family member taking him to his first match in the early seventies whilst he was at a young and impressionable age Andy Rivers discovered Newcastle United. Given the stress and despair this has caused him over the last thirty years it's fair to assume that this action would be considered child abuse today. His story, peppered with terrace wit and rough charm, will be identified with by supporters of a certain age everywhere.

Released Aug '09 - The book Nick Hornby should've bloody wrote!

A LIFE OF TWO HALVES
MORE BURGLAR DIARIES

Danny King

Bex and Ollie are a couple of small time burglars. They scratch a living robbing shops, burgling factories and emptying offices around the back water town of Tatley. Bex is the brains, Ollie drives the van.

The lads don't have it all their own way though; 'Weasel' of CID is only one step behind them, the local competition will do anything to spike them and the loves of their lives are wondering what they've done to deserve them.

Things are about to finally catch up with Bex and Ollie.

THIEVES LIKE US

Released Dec '09...Get it in ya stocking!

See the website for more details www.bykerbooks.co.uk

Printed in the United Kingdom by
Lightning Source UK Ltd., Milton Keynes
140738UK00001B/70/P

9 780956 078834